Praise for *My Happy Life*

"Millet's last novel, *George Bush, Dark Prince of Love*, was a sharply comic study in delusion, her newest, a miracle of linguistic compression laced with venomous irony. . . . Millet's shocking yet poetic tale of survival in a cruel world, enlightenment, and transcendence will rock readers to their very core."—*Booklist*

"Occasionally a book comes along that is truly written (as writers are instructed books should be) as if it were the writer's last: Millet's sad and infinitely touching third novel (after the absurdist *George Bush, Dark Prince of Love*) is such an extraordinary work. . . . A courageous and memorable achievement."
—*Publishers Weekly*

"Strange and incandescent. . . . Millet's two previous novels were bizarre and wonderfully inventive. . . . [*My Happy Life*] is absurd. It's also beautiful, and achieving that unlikely balance is a prodigious feat. . . . A sharp and frequently funny novel."— *New York Times Book Review*

"Millet's third novel is a nightmare lined in gold."
—*Entertainment Weekly*

"Lydia Millet . . . strips life down to its simplest components in her strange and lovely new novel. . . . Quirky and ethereal."—*Village Voice*

"Millet's prose is spare and elegant. . . . A heart-rending novel."—*Boston Herald*

Praise for *George Bush, Dark Prince of Love*

"An insanely funny novel with a savagely wicked bite."
—*New York Daily News*

"Set against the backdrop of the George Bush presidential years, Lydia Millet's *George Bush, Dark Prince of Love* is the most sardonic and laugh-out-loud funny satire I've read in years."—*Denver Rocky Mountain News*

"Part fable, part farce, 'Dark Prince' is one of the freshest books I've read on modern politics."
—*Raleigh News and Observer*

Praise for *Omnivores*

"If Flannery O'Connor came back from the dead and abandoned her fixation with Southern religion, she might be proud to write something like Lydia Millet's astonishing first novel, *Omnivores*."
—*Fort Lauderdale Sun-Sentinel*

"All manner of voracious American appetites—for sex, power, and possessions—are darkly lampooned in this strange, often very funny debut."
—*Entertainment Weekly*

EVERYONE'S PRETTY

EVERYONE'S PRETTY

LYDIA MILLET

SOFT SKULL PRESS
BROOKLYN, NEW YORK
2005

Everyone's Pretty
ISBN: 1-932360-77-8
©2005 by Lydia Millet

Cover Design by David Janik
ShortLit Series Design by David Janik and Charles Orr

Published by Soft Skull Press • www.softskull.com
Distributed by Publishers Group West • www.pgw.com

Printed in the U.S.A.

Cataloging-in-Publication data for this title is available from
the Library of Congress.

CHAPTER THE FIRST

Introducing a Prince among men,
a Holy Woman, and a sheep

TUESDAY EVENING
10:11

Fat men were often powerful, that was true. Their girth did not appear unseemly, flanked by the pillars and arches of state. Thin men, however, were the revolutionaries and the seers. Che Guevara was not been a corpulent man, nor was Mahatma Gandhi. Also, the thin ones lived longer. Emaciation and longevity went hand in hand. For this reason Decetes had, from time to time, considered a regimen of starvation, but he was always too hungry. —Now I will starve, he would say, and his resolve would carry him from one day to the next. Then there would be his stomach, an abandoned child. He took pity on it.

Still, he knew the pride of self-restraint. A thin man was a lone wolf on the prowl.

Decetes applied himself to reading the graffiti on the toilet stall. He was an amateur archaeologist—or perhaps, since he rarely dug holes in the ground, merely an anthropologist.

For he often studied mankind. Yes, he devoted himself to their study, so he could better know them.

Know thine enemy, it was said.

I fucked yer sister, read one line. In another script beneath this, *Go home Dad your drunk.*

Decetes admired the homespun candor. It was here, above the rust-washed urinals, across the slate-gray metal doors of public bodily relief, that the psyche of the underclass found unfettered expression. The underclass was canny and astute. Decetes lauded their efforts.

He was hiding out in the restroom after a minor altercation with another bar patron, who had threatened him with injury. —Len, pour me another one, he had said. That was all. A not unreasonable request. —You've had enough, said Len. Len was not the garrulous, hearty bartender glorified by urban folklore. Len kept himself to himself. At times his surly furtiveness was irritating. Decetes had acquired the habit of poking at Len with the stick of his banter, trying to nudge him out of his hole.

But Len, like all burrowers, could dig himself quite deep beneath the surface. He had reached up for a bottle of Gordon's and poured a drink for someone else. Decetes had to follow his course to the end. —Len, you will pour me another one, or my army will roust your family from its home, rape the children and plunder the women. We will steal your valuables Len, and write with blood on the walls.

Sadly Len had no sense of humor. And Len had friends among the other regulars.

Decetes opened the restroom door slowly, eyed the exit sign and stealthily made his move, slinking low like a cat. Yes! He set off down the street in the dark. Houses started up: the block became residential not fifty steps away from The Quiet Man. Here was a well-lit house with people drinking on the front lawn. A fresh and gratis keg, wellspring of liquid truth? Possibly. He would investigate. Some of the people outside stood drinking from clear plastic cups: a favorable sign. A blond woman in a short-sleeved minidress chafed one bare arm with the other hand as he walked past. Scantily clad, the floozy! Bless her soul.

He would talk to her later, drink in hand.

He headed up the front walk, a placating smile to his right and to his left in case the host was present. He waved an eager hand, as though catching sight of a friend, and mounted the porch steps two at a time. There it was: the Grail, on the hardwood living-room floor. A man in a pink shirt stooped over its tin spout, cup tipped almost horizontal, manipulating the hose with a deftness familiar to Decetes. The keg was low. He had arrived in the nick of time. He removed a clean cup from the top of a pile.

—You would be? asked someone. He turned to face the interloper. It was a severe looking woman with glasses and short hair. Her long skirt bore a pattern of flying ducks.

—Dean Decetes, friend of John's, he said easily, and held out his hand for her to shake.

— . . . Ramon's friend? she asked. —I'm Darlene.

He was already at the spout.

—Nice place here, he said. Bent over the keg, he was at her waist level. The bulge of an abdomen constricted by cotton. Distracted by a shriek from the rear of the house, she passed him by. The ducks were flying south for the winter. Clutching his cup, heavy with tepid Miller Genuine Draft, he followed her back to the bedroom area, whence came the shriek that augured free entertainment. Where humbler men would have hedged and tiptoed, Decetes strode with confidence. His gatecrashing skills had been honed through the lean years, and were now at their apex.

A porcine man stood at the bedroom door. He too was an onlooker. A cigarette drooped from his mouth.

—Bum a smoke? asked Decetes.

—All out, said the fat man, and retreated grunting.

Decetes peered into the bedroom. On a double bed a man lay on his stomach, with his pants around his knees. Darlene the duck lover bent over him and another woman hovered with her hands fluttering. Decetes ambled closer, taking a swig from his cup, and peered down. The man's bare buttocks were awash with blood. A gaping wound at the top of his crack was flowing freely.

—Vince what were you thinking? asked Darlene. —Surgery two days ago and he dances. Of course the suture's going to split.

She looked up.

—Stand back, said Decetes. —I'm an emergency medical technician.

Many guises wore the Holy One.

—What a coincidence! said the other woman. Her lipstick was smeared. —It's like hemorrhaging!

—Gotta ice pack? queried Decetes. Authoritative. —Put some ice on there. It's not serious.

—Let me check the freezer, said Darlene, on her way out the door.

—Are just regular cubes okay?

—Ice is ice, lady, said Decetes with calm contempt. He didn't like the man's looks. His face was ashen and he had thick lips. It figured. He strolled in off the street and right up to a man's bloody rectum. It was the luck of the Irish, though Decetes was certainly no Mick.

He chuckled and gave the guy a rough pat to the shoulder. —You'll be fine, bud, he said.

—He had a cyst removed, said the woman with lipstick. —Benign, but it was causing him discomfort.

—They'll do that, said Decetes. —A cyst will do that. I'm no big fan of cysts. Personally, I can take 'em or leave 'em.

—You're an EMT? asked the bloody man. The side of his flabby face was pressed into the pillow. —Where'd you get your certification?

—UCLA Medical School, said Decetes. —Back in '83. Career change since then, but I still know my stuff.

—Hey. Are you even sober?

—Here we go, announced Darlene, bustling in with a handful of ice in a rag. —Hold tight there Vince. We're all here for you.

—Has that been sterilized, duck-lover? Decetes asked her sternly.

—Huh? No but it's clean, she protested.

Decetes shook his head firmly.

—Uh uh uh, he intoned. —Paper towels are the way to go.

She exited again.

—I didn't know they had EMT training courses at UCLA, said Vince.

—Learn something new every day, said Decetes. He had taken control, yet the beneficiary of his baronial goodwill was ungrateful. It was too frequently the case. Ingrates peopled the earth in obscene abundance. He quit the room, tapped the keg for a final few drops and went outside.

The blond floozy had a jacket draped over her shoulders. It had evidently been donated by the man shivering beside her in his T-shirt. P-whipped. Decetes approached them with a sure step; yet it was too sure. He tripped over a flagstone and toppled into the woman, spilling his beer on her chest and arm as they crashed to the ground.

—Christ, said the wimp in the T-shirt, extending a sallow hand to raise his pom-pom girl from the compacted turf. She was pinned beneath Decetes and he did not willingly relinquish his position. Through her thin dress he felt hillocks and valleys. It was a frontal paradise, a lush country.

Decetes was becoming aroused.

—Get off me, she ground out through clenched teeth, and pushed against his chest with her palms. Decetes dared to hope she had not noticed his tumescence.

—Sorry, I was stunned, he said, and raised himself onto all fours. The woman struggled from beneath him, scooting backward on the ground. He saw her legs. They were tanned and slim, though imperfectly shaven.

—Stunned? You had an erection!

—Madam, you presume. I am a man with high standards. That was my lighter you felt, said Decetes.

—Big goddamn lighter, she said, and picked grass off her arm.

—Shaped like a mushroom.

—Alice, let's just go, said the ninety-eight-pound weakling, stooping to pick up his jacket.

—Jesus, said Alice, squinting at Decetes. —I know you.

—You know him?

—You're Bucella's brother, the one who was falling down drunk at Thanksgiving. I saw you fall onto a poker.

—Bucella is my sister, yes. But water is thicker than blood.

—I work with Bucella. Alice Reeve. This is Lonn.

She reached out to shake his hand, but he was patting his pockets as though for a business card. There were none in existence, of course.

—Dean Decetes.

—We're in AA, said Lonn stiffly. —I'm Alice's sponsor. I think you should consider joining us at the next meeting. On Wilshire, near Lincoln.

—Oh ho, oh ho, said Decetes, withdrawing his hand to raise it in protest. —Missionaries, zealots. Proselytists! Please leave me. I would be alone. Peddle your picture Bibles elsewhere. I am content to dance my heathen dances and sharpen my weapons on stones.

—One day you'll be ready, said Lonn.

—That'll be the day-hey-hey when I die, said Decetes. —I know your kind. You bring religion and you take away the wealth. You and your fellow pioneers are waging war upon my people, but for now I will hold out. I have my savage rapture and my ancestral lands. Goodnight sweet ladies. The keg has been duly drained. Me and my mushroom make our merry way home. Fungus, bungus, fungus. Hale fellows well met.

Four houses later, he positioned himself at the base of a dying jacaranda and unleashed himself upon the weeds. As he craned his neck to study the sky his trajectory altered, spraying porch, soil and doormat. Glancing back at the party on the lawn, he saw a bespectacled woman twirling shirtless on the sidewalk and regretted his early departure. But it was a barren waste there, breeding no Miller out of the dead land. And the lilacs could fuck off.

10:57

—That woman is troubled, said Lonn. —We should help her.

—I don't think it's really our business, said Alice. —Maybe she's just having a good time.

They watched as the woman, glasses askew on her face, flapped her arms and danced giddily on the pavement, a solitary dervish. Alice stared at the breasts, drooping pears slinging right and left. The woman had her eyes closed, and her mouth hung open.

—Babs, honey, come in now, rushed Darlene, coming down the front steps. —Honey, you need to rest. Come on in with big sister.

—I'm a streaker, squeaked Babs. —I'm a belly dancer!

—Come on now.

—I'm going to the little boys' room, said Lonn, and followed them inside.

—Little boys' room?

Lonn made her wince on a regular basis. He was the author of many winces a day.

She sat down on a step and lit a cigarette, thinking of Bucella's drunken brother. He was a puffy vagabond, a staggering W.C. Fields rated XXX. Minus the dignity. But regardless of the source, insults bored beneath her skin and laid their eggs. She could never disregard a cruel word; for all she knew Bucella's drunken brother was an idiot savant. For all she knew he was right, she *had* turned into a sheep. Maybe she *was* walking in circles with her nose in a feedbag. Maybe one day she would drop from exhaustion; cloven hooves would flatten her fleecy carcass.

Guests chattered and nodded. There was the illusion of contact, but she was always untouched. They talked about one of two subjects: themselves or nothing at all. It had been years since people surprised her.

The end of routine, that would be the only surprise.

A laughing woman came out the front door, tapping Alice's back with a raised foot as she stumbled down the steps. —Oh that's so interesting! she squealed at the man behind her.

—What is interesting? What the fuck is *interesting?* said Alice, and crushed her Camel butt on the wooden porch as she stood. It fell between the slats, sparking. The woman giggled, the man shrugged whispering a word—*bitch*—as Alice walked past, and she was clear of them. The faces changed but not the quality of light beneath them, the dim flat light. And she was static too, like the rest, always a disappointment. She made light into silence.

Sobriety was like this: useless. What did you do to tempt yourself onward? Where was the carrot?

She walked away. Lonn could wander the place looking for her; it would keep him busy.

At the corner of the street was a dive called The Quiet Man. Inside, in the dark, she could barely make out a pool table, a jukebox and a burly bearded man in leather vest and turbulent chest hair with a parrot on his shoulder. He was doing shots at the counter. She sat down two stools away and ordered a club soda.

—Jack the Sailor, ask Len for another Kamikaze, said the man with the parrot, and belched.

—Get this man a drink, squawked the parrot.

—Coming right up, said the barkeep.

—Good boy Jack the Sailor, said the man, and fed the parrot a peanut from his pocket.

—What else can he say, said Alice.

—Shut up Juanita, said the parrot. —You goddamn two-dollar Mexican whore.

—I see.

—Don't take it the wrong way, said Jack the Sailor's owner, stroking the feathered head. —He had a bad childhood. The club soda's on me.

Alice smiled at him. He did not smile back, but he would smile soon.

She envied beehives and anthills. The glue of instinct kept them together, and they did not lie alone in the dark.

Having rested for an interlude between a Dumpster and a fence, Decetes staggered toward his Pinto as sirens shrieked and a fire truck careened past, narrowly missing his foot. He took a swig from his half-empty fifth of Black Label, turned the key in the ignition and talked to himself as he drove. — Greater love hath no man than this, that he should lay down his wife for his friend.

Soon a black-and-white flashed its bawdy colors behind him. Decetes considered the options, which included a high-speed chase; but the time was not right. He pulled over and was subjected to an informal test. Toes, toes, wherefore art thou, unseemly digits? They were, sadly, beyond his reach. He was no longer the young and limber cavalier of former days. Black holes! The universe contracted like an angry sphincter.

He collapsed onto the street.

—Officer, he said when he was able to sit up, —this is not necessary. I'm way below the legal limit. One beer, that's it. My father was a member of the Temperance League. We are Mormons. To a man.

—Sir, your license has been suspended twice for this offense, said the cop.

Sir? The cop was clearly a rookie. Decetes saw him graduating from high school not two years ago, a mortarboard askew atop his pimpled brow, and decided to implement Plan A.

—Listen Officer, maybe you'll take an interest in my work. I'm a freelance editor, said Decetes. —Review movies for a national magazine. Fact you may be familiar with some of our publications.

The rookie let him bring out a copy from the backseat, but one look at the nudity inside and Decetes's ass was grass. The officer was a fundamentalist Christian of some stripe, clearly. Perhaps a Promise Keeper, even. Family values up the wazoo.

—We also publish a magazine for the law-enforcement community, fact I've done quite a lot of writing for it, started Decetes, reaching for the gun magazines spilled over the vinyl. But his hands were cuffed behind him in a trice. If he was not greatly mistaken they would be suspending his license for good.

In the squad car he attempted to draw the rookie out on the subject of value systems.

—Are you of the Pentecostal persuasion? he asked. —Your brother or father handle snakes? Snake-handling in the family? I handle one myself. Frequently.

—Shut up, please.

—Your sister speak in tongues? Glossolalia? My sister does. Once a month on the rag. I'm not kidding. Armenian, Swedish, what have you. Officer, I swear to the good Lord it's true. You should come over and hear her sometime. I can get you in free of charge.

—Shut up! snapped the rookie again, agitated. His radio was squawking out an emergency. He picked it up, spoke into it and spun the wheel.

—I have to take a leak, I'm going to mess up your upholstery here, said Decetes.

They pulled up behind two fire trucks. The house previously visited by Decetes was ablaze. A small crowd milled in the street; into the night air triumphant arcs of water spewed. Decetes was reminded of his needs.

—Don't leave me here Officer, he begged. —I'll piss on the seat. Leave the cuffs on, just let me take a leak. You think a man in my condition could get far? You have my license Officer.

—All right, just shut up I told you, said the rookie in a high-pitched voice, sweating profusely. He popped the back door open and ran toward the firefighters. Decetes opened his flies to the gutter, looked over his shoulder at the cop and then wended down a driveway and through someone's backyard.

The Pinto was elsewhere. He called home from a payphone.

—There's a possibility, he said, —the Los Angeles Police Department may have impounded my vehicle.

—Not again, you lowlife, said Bucella.

—Just pick me up, he said.

—Forget it, said Bucella. —I told you, the next DUI I do not bail you out.

—Wait, wait, said Decetes. —No bailing, no nothing. I'm here in my shirtsleeves on the side of the road.

—So what, said Bucella. —You have legs.

—I may meet with physical harm, said Decetes. —There are several potential assailants in the area. I mean here I am on a dark street with homeless individuals and African-Americans hooked on crack cocaine.

—You're a racist Dean, said Bucella.

—Racist, schmacist. I tell it like it is. This isn't Disneyland Bucella. Do you want to be responsible for my stabbing death? Here I am with a guy who I think may have a switchblade, Bucella. He smells like a 40-ounce. He's coming closer. Jesus. He's here! Oh help Bucella! Help!

—I'm sure you'll hit it off, said Bucella. —No means no. She hung up.

—Goddamn Bucella, said Decetes aloud. —Not worth the ribonuke—oxyribe— . . . DNA she's made of.

There was no one to hear him, since the street, which was well-lit by the orange glow on the horizon, housed no vagrants or addicts. He wrested a broken cigarette from his pocket, the cuffs chafing his wrists, and lit it. Pinching it tightly at the fissure, he started off in the direction of Santa Monica Boulevard, to catch a bus. But then he stopped in his tracks. Something had captured his attention. He stood swaying and gazed up at the firmament. Vast it was, but void of stars. Instead of celestial bodies the night sky was dappled with representations of his own face. How benevolent, how like a God! But how human. He was willing to admit it. A patriot and an American.

—A patriot, sir, and an American.

Let them come! His weapons were invisible but potent. His armaments were splendid. For he had what other men could only dream of having: a conscience clear as firewater.

11:55

Bucella had been organizing her spice rack when Dean so rudely interrupted. Each spice was numbered. A1 was garlic, B1 was basil, C1 was cilantro, D1 was rosemary, E1 was oregano. She classified them by frequency of use, with subheadings for variations on a theme. A2 was garlic salt. And she had a new plan: from now on she would lock the cupboard to prevent her brother from wreaking havoc among the Innocent Herbs.

With Dean around the house she had no Future, that was clear. He was like a maimed old dog squatting on the floor, flatulent. Decent people pitied him but they also feared him. At Thanksgiving he had fallen on his face when he carried in the cranberry sauce. He was always falling. He fell when he had nothing else to do. It was the closest thing he knew to a party trick. —Does your brother have a drinking problem? Alice Reeve had asked when he'd gone back to the kitchen for a wet cloth. —Yes he does, said Bucella. —He does have a drinking problem. It's a classic case. He has a problem and he won't let me help.

But Dean was back quicker than she'd expected and caught the end of her sentence.

—My drinking is not a problem, he announced to the assembled Company. —It is an avocation. I turn wine into water. I am an alchemist and a magician.

Ten minutes later he got up to go to the bathroom, tripped on the rug and gouged a hole in his cheek. It was a poker from the stand beside the fireplace. —Fall-o-Matic, whispered Alice Reeve, within Bucella's hearing. If Bucella recalled correctly, Alice had been none too sober herself. That was before she started going to AA. Now she wasn't a drunkard anymore, that was true, but she had myriad other Flaws. Though friendly, Alice was a Loose Woman. She gave of Herself too freely. Jesus wept.

Bucella scrubbed a burner ring with steel wool. Ernest Lesser had become agitated when the poker went through Dean's face. Bucella had noticed and bustled around in a demonstration of Caring, though she had seen much worse. She had seen her brother perform an Obscene Act upon the end of an arrow when he was in his Cups, and then fall on the arrow, which pierced the roof of his mouth and adorned him with a Beard of Blood. He had not even noticed the blood until she pointed it out.

But this time, for Ernest's sake, she had guided Dean to the kitchen and tended to him like Florence Nightingale.

Later, when she and Ernest stood talking by the mantelpiece, Dean had approached them weaving and made disparaging remarks about her choice of wine. He said it was a California table wine and a ripoff at $2.99. Which was not true since it was Beaujolais from France, $5.99 on special sale. Then Dean asked Ernest right out loud what he himself thought about Ribbed Prophylactics. —Myself I never use 'em, said Dean. —Double Her Pleasure while I'm fucking latex, perish the thought. Many women do not realize that the nerve endings in the penis are less sensitive than the nerves in the fingertips. The penis has a sensitivity that is largely overrated. Your average penis is deaf, dumb and blind. Your average penis has the sensitivity of a liverwurst.

He paused, then continued.

—I am referring, of course, to the shaft.

Bucella had gone running to the kitchen. She stood at the sink washing plates, trying not to cry till Dean stumbled in and tried to pee in the trashcan.

—There's someone in the head, my bladder's bursting, he said, but she beat him about the shoulders with a spatula until he left the garbage can alone, saying *Foul Demon! Foul Demon!*

Then she blew her nose, dried her eyes and was gracious again to Ernest, dignified in her Adversity.

Once the guests had gone she gave Dean a serious lecture.

—I work with these people, she said. —I try to cultivate mutual respect!

Dean had folded back the pages of the Vile Pornographic Publication he was reading as she averted her gaze. He looked up from the Naked Hussy and cocked an eyebrow at Bucella. —Respect? Sure, he said. —I respect the hell outta this girl. Excuse me. I have business in my room.

She would have to hire a carpenter to put a lock onto the spice cabinet. That would take until Monday or Tuesday. But maybe Dean wouldn't notice the numbers and wouldn't disturb anything. He never used spices. When he cooked it was at three in the morning, packaged Ramen with MSG. She walked to the den. There were piles of crushed beer cans and X-rated movies on Dean's table in front of the VCR. She could not help noticing the Rude and Profane titles. *Buttman Goes to Rio. Bend Over Babes 3. Sodomania 1.* He sat there two nights a week with the remote control, pretending to evaluate the movies for his Sordid Tabloid. At these times she avoided the room, since she had interrupted him once with his zipper open, Exposed.

Her brother blundered in, kicking over a rattling object, and slammed the door behind him. She went back to the kitchen to finish cleaning. He stumbled over the floor with a cigarette butt dangling from his lips, his hands cuffed together, and opened the refrigerator.

He smelled bad, very bad. Like a dead weasel would.

—You're not smoking in the house, she cautioned, but he ignored her, closing the refrigerator and extracting a moldy heel of bread from his personal supply in the breadbin. He removed the cigarette from his mouth, dropped it into the sink and bit into the bread. —What are those things doing on your hands? Don't leave that butt in the sink either, she ordered, and exited the kitchen. Dean stuck up his middle finger as she turned her back. He had always been grossly Vulgar.

When she went back to the den he followed her. She sat down and turned on the news. He perched on the arm of the couch.

—Think you could cut these things off with a power tool?

—I could, she said stiffly. —But *would* I.

—I'll make a mess if I try to do it myself. I could hack off a finger by mistake. Then you'd have to drive me to the hospital.

—Change out of those filthy clothes why don't you, said Bucella. —Because you really smell.

He unbuttoned his shirt. Bucella stared straight ahead at the screen.

—Bucella I'm disappointed in you, said her brother. —I could have been killed. I barely escaped with my life.

—Don't lie, said Bucella, changing the channel.

—You think I exaggerate? I went to a Versateller to get some money out, guy sleeping on the ground grabbed onto my ankle. Tried to gnaw through the tendon. It's an act of divine intervention I've still got the use of my lower body. Had to give him forty bucks to get off me.

—Show me the scar then, said Bucella.

—What, I'm supposed to have stigmata now? It was my pants he was biting into, it's lucky he didn't get through to the skin. Five more seconds I would have been maimed. See Bucella I divested myself, he crawled away with the bills. Had his saliva on my cuff for ten full minutes before it dried.

—You have no shame, said Bucella. —Now would you leave me alone? I'm trying to watch this program.

—Bucella Bucella, said Dean, shaking his head. He retreated to the kitchen and she heard cupboard doors opening and closing. Finally he reappeared with her ground cinnamon in his hand.

—Put that back, she told him harshly.

—What is this, all the spices have letters and numbers?

—Just put it back, she said. —Right where you got it. I mean it.

—Jesus Bucella, this is what you had to do, this is what I risked my life for out there? For this I could have been thrown into the pokey and raped by a convict?

—I'd like to see the convict that would rape you.

—I believe I will hold this cinnamon hostage.

—Put it back Dean. Right now.

—My ransom demand shall be as follows. You must cut these primitive restraints off my hands with a tool from the basement. If you do this immediately I will release the cinnamon into your custody.

—Shut up, said Bucella. —Maybe later if you're good.

Decetes padded back into the kitchen, where she heard him fall with a clatter to the floor.

She turned off the TV. He had passed out; there was a broken glass beside him on the linoleum. Luckily the cinnamon had rolled under the dishwasher and was unharmed. She returned it to the cabinet and mounted the stairs to her bedroom.

On her back, toes stretched out beneath the taut covers, she cleared her mind of her brother's detritus and placed Ernest at the end of a tunnel. Behind him there was Light. He wore a loincloth and a Crown of Thorns. —Bucella, he said, his voice grave. —Wash my feet.

She fell to the ground and washed them, bathing them in kisses. The skin was tender and smelled sweet. The legs of Ernest rose like sinewed columns, like graceful Greek statues, the Colossus of Rhodes. He bent and placed a strong, dry hand on her head.

—Rise, Bucella, he said, and when she got to her feet, her cheeks wet with tears of joy, he lifted her up and strode with her to the shadows.

CHAPTER THE SECOND

All greet the day with new Hope; Dreams are dreamed
and Love is declared; and public morals are examined.
Introducing an Innocent and an Honest Man

WEDNESDAY MORNING
3:11

When he woke up on the kitchen floor, Decetes lay gazing at the linoleum. He was plagued by a question. Who would play him in the movie? There was no one of suitable stature. In days of yore, Charlton Heston might have been selected. He had played Moses. But since then he'd been exposed as a bad actor and a Republican.

Possibly he, Decetes, would be called upon to play himself in his life story. It would be an irritation, like flies on an elephant, but he would consent to make time for the task. This was his burden. He took it into account. Yes: a movie of his life story.

However, the path to glory was obscured for the moment. It had slipped his mind. It would return, no doubt.

He hauled himself up, unsteady. His wrists were raw and bleeding from the cuffs. After a moment of rushing nausea gravity raised its dizzying anchor and he was upright, a hand on the sink edge, feet planted far apart on terra firma. He lifted his hands and shaded his brow: was it land there, in the distance? Was he a conquistador with Incan gold off the starboard bow, and wild animals to kill?

It was the moldy loaf in dishwater, surmounted by the white corpse of a Marlboro.

In Bucella's study he opened a file cabinet and moved a few papers from a folder named Taxes 1996 to a folder named Taxes 2005. Into each life some rain must fall. Unlike his law-abiding sister, he himself had no truck with taxation agencies. As men searched in perpetuity for God and failed to pinpoint his location, so fared the IRS with Dean Decetes.

He noticed a Post-It note on Bucella's desk: *Mrs. Ernest Lesser. Bucella D. Lesser.* She had done the same thing when she was 11, imagining herself in connubial bliss with a shrimpy sixth-grader named Davy. Decetes had given her an Indian sunburn then, twisting the skin on her wrist until she was forced to repeat after him, —Davy and Bucella, sitting in a tree, F-U-C-K-I-N-G.

He detached the Post-It from its pad and stuck it on one of Bucella's religious prints on the wall: *Triptych of the Annunciation, Robert Campin, Flemish, d.1444.* It pictured an old geezer doing carpentry, a fat sow reading a picture book and a faggot angel overturning a table. Bucella had acquired it recently, attempting to get culture in the gift shop of the L.A. County Museum.

Yes, he was a man with an ambitious plan. To work, to work. He reclined in the viewing throne, wielded the remote in a kingly fist and watched two double penetrations in a row. He must be brought before the masses of the unwashed.

He had denied the inklings of his destiny for long enough, for even through adversity he always had been certain: Dean Decetes was not just a man.

The means might be persuasion, or they might be force. Force required manpower, armed to the teeth. In the legions of his army, he would need a loyal footsoldier. Recruitment was one of his many talents, fortunately. He had found his first convert, and a man-at-arms would soon be his. It was an acolyte, a worshipper. A fanatical reader of the scriptures of smut, an assault-with-a-deadly whose Bible was porn. His day was nigh, and its name was parole.

When they had briefly shared a cell in lockup, Ken had been deeply impressed by the sight of Decetes's name on the printed page, beneath a review of an amateur girl-girl video titled *Furpie Frenzy*. Swiftly Decetes had reeled him in, a fish on a hook. As a result, soon Decetes would no longer be a solitary visionary but a revolutionary general with five stars, albeit self-conferred. Ken would be his first Private.

He fast-forwarded through dialogue, stopping only when flesh filled the screen. With his hands chained together, it was unfortunately a choice, at any given moment, between the pen and the wand. Notations on his yellow foolscap took form slowly, painstakingly. *2 DPs, Madison, Sierra w/ Rocco Siffredi & Hedgehog; 3 anal, Alicyn Sterling, Tianna and Alicia Rio; 2 Girl-Girl.* A long pause for refreshment; then, vigor renewed, back into the fray. *Enema scene.*

4:57

Bucella woke up from disturbed sleep, her back aching. She had been dreaming about seraphim, the highest order of Angels. They were six-winged and stood in the presence of the Almighty, but their backs were riddled with craters and speckled with black hair. They were emaciated and drooling, with concave blue-veined chests. They were her tormentors. They came to stick pins in her sleep, their sharpened teeth sparkling in the dark, their hoary paws grabbing at her with curling claws clicking and scratching, leaving a gray film where they walked. She slid, slipped and fell turning and twisting as they screeched. She pushed back the comforter and got out of bed.

It was Dean's fault. Her brother made the Angels ugly. Downstairs he was dozing in his chair with the remote control loosely clasped in one cuffed hand. She removed it, noting the lines of dirt beneath his square nails, the yellow swirls of his nicotine fingerprints. A legal pad lay on the floor. He had written the words *giant gazongas*. Typical, Repulsive.

Her Post-It note was stuck onto the framed print on the wall. She snatched it off. Dean could do his worst. His taunts were the lashes of Lucifer himself, but she could withstand them. The martyrs had suffered In Extremis.

She leaned over and peered at him again. His mouth was hanging open. Spittle was brimming inside the rim of the lower lip—against the gums riddled, as she had not been pleased to notice, with Periodontal Disease. She had urged him to visit the dentist, but he would not take her advice. An ounce of prevention was too much for Dean. Before long his teeth would be exposed down to their roots, and would fall from the disintegrating tissue like confetti at a wedding.

Dean was her cross to bear. Tribulations had to be endured. They would strengthen her for her Tasks.

She switched off the light and went to the dining room, where her book *Revelations of Divine Love* lay open on a floral placemat. All shall be well, and all manner of things shall be well, she read aloud. She traced her finger over the pattern of a daisy on the placemat, following the line of its bright-green stem.

—Unshackle me, woman, growled Dean, staggering in from the den. He stood slumping in front of her, slack-jawed.

—Shut up, said Bucella. —You don't deserve it.

She stared down at the pages, pretending concentration. *The ebbing away of my life,* read the typed words, but though she held them firm, unwavering before her eyes, all she could think of was her brother's rancid odor. Blood of my blood, flesh of my flesh, you stink. Julian of Norwich had seen sixteen showings of God, but was also visited by a Demon, who put his claws on her throat and pushed his foul-smelling face into hers.

Bucella smiled privately, her throat clenched. After a minute the Demon turned, leaned down to pick a magazine off the floor awkwardly with his hands still cuffed together, and left the room.

One day Jesus and the Virgin would glide across the sun in a golden Chariot and flocks of saints would fly behind them in a Shimmering Parade. And all the children and the nice people could go with them. And far above in Paradise, Bucella and Ernest would be united in Matrimony to organ strains.

Dean could go right on down to hell to be with his Fornicating Friends. He enjoyed himself most in the company of Ladies of the Evening and Slimy Pimps. Oh yes, he would be perfectly happy there, lying in Burning Coals and Damned Eternal Flames wiggling his Member.

But then—Mercy—if he stopped being a Drunkard he could wash himself clean of Foul Things and, like Venus in that painting where she was almost naked on the lily pad which was not filthy since it certainly was Art, rise from the waves. He could be rejuvenated, innocent as a newborn. There might still be room for him on the rolling dales of Heaven.

She faced east through the dining room window, gazing at the pale bands of color on the horizon, violet and pink. In the blink of an eye she saw herself and Ernest on a wide, white marble verandah, filmed through a breathed-on lens. Ernest's arm was around her, and they watched from the doors of their Pearly Mansion with proud tears in their eyes as Dean, reborn, a little boy of eight again, squatted on the vast green hill in the mist of morning, among the many Wildflowers in the Fields, beating a march on a tiny toy drum and smiling to himself.

7:01

Dawn was the hour when cocks best liked to crow. Decetes put aside his labors and headed upstairs, to the small window on the landing between flights. It provided a view of the second-floor bedroom next door. Like clockwork! There she was—standing, stretching, her lean nubile limbs bleached by rays of early sunlight, in pink satiny brassiere and nothing else. Her back was to him. The buttocks were hills of snow, smooth as butter, a smiling face. The furry chops of a kitten. Then she turned, baring all, leaned out and glared at him.

—Fuck off you old lech, she said. —I'll tell my mother. You get on my nerves.

—Turn the other cheek, said Decetes.

—Shut your trap, she retorted.

—A word to the wise, said Decetes. —Two can play at that game. Your poor dear mother would not be pleased to learn of your nocturnal habits.

He had seen her entertain a gangbanger in her bedroom on several occasions. The kid commonly snuck out through the window when they were done, and drove away in a lowrider with a purple crown-shaped deodorizer in the rear window.

—Go play golf with your senile friends, she said, and reached up to unfurl the fake Venetian blind.

But Decetes already had what he needed. Stimulus, from the Latin root *stimulare*. Thankfully, he was gifted with perfect visual recall. He headed back down to the den.

7:08

Rat-a-tat-tat came the knock at her bedroom door. She knelt and grabbed the black Trojan wrapper, crumpling it in her hand.

—Ginny?

The door opened, and there was her mother in the ugly orange-pink velvet dressing gown stained with dried egg yolk. It was actually gross.

—I'm naked!

—I'm sorry honey.

—I didn't say come in! You promised!

—Who were you talking to?

—I said get out! I'm naked!

Ignore. Ignore.

—Ginny I heard you talking.

—Would you get out of my room? This is my private room!

—Ginny I want to know who you were talking to.

Logarithm .01, -4.60517, logarithm .02, -3.91202, logarithm .03, .50656. She computed quickly, pulling on her miniskirt with closed eyes and the Trojan wrapper still in her hand. *Logarithm .04, .21888, logarithm .05, -2.99573.*

—Do you hear me? Answer me Ginny!

—Logarithm .4, -0.91629, she said out loud, and snapped the bra closed. —Logarithm .41, .8916. Logarithm—

—Stop it! Stop that math! I'm asking you, was that perverted child molester talking to you through the window again?

—No one was talking to me, I was talking to myself! I was doing math! Okay?

—Honey okay, but remember what the man from the gifted program said—

—Shut up!

—You could go there for free. And be with other gifteds.

—Those places are for geeks.

—He said you would have your own peer group. He said there were other gifteds your age. Honey I'm sure once you got there—

—Get out! Out out out!

—I have your breakfast ready honey.

—Goddamn logarithm 1.24, .21511, log 1.25, .22314—

—Okay honey, see you downstairs. You have to eat Ginny. I mean it.

Ginny scrounged around in her knapsack for the strawberry lipgloss and applied it, pouting into the mirror. Her door was clearly labeled POLICE LINE DO NOT CROSS, in bright yellow tape, but her mother was obviously colorblind to yellow. She poked into the room like a starving mutt sniffing at stinky garbage. Only the Terminator could stop her.

One night Ginny would smuggle him in and hide him behind the door. Then, when her mother pushed the door open, wearing her velvet robe and the slippers shaped like pink rabbits, and said "Honey? Did I hear something?" Arnold Schwarzenegger would step out, the bad Terminator not the good one, with a gigantic machine gun in his arms.

His red eyes would be gleaming. He would grin so you could see the evil gap between his teeth, say "Die Bitch" in that fake German accent and mow her down.

Later the bullets would turn out to be blanks and she would be stunned but unharmed. She needed electric-shock therapy to teach her a lesson. After the meeting with the Terminator she would be a whole new woman and never irritating again.

Right now everything went in one ear and out the other. It was like there was a chute between the ears, with the ball of words rolling along the chute to drop out and land on the shoulder of the dirty orange robe. If one ear was half a centimeter higher than the other and her mother's head was seven inches wide, or 17.78 cm in metric, the length of the chute was the square root of 316.3784, which equaled 17.787. Acceleration of the ball of words was very slow. The ball rolled through her mother's head at a near-constant speed. But then gravity was 9.806 meters per second.

Maybe the head was more than seven inches wide. But to measure it she would have to touch her mother. Vomit vomit. As if.

After six coats the lipgloss was perfect. Eyeliner was harder. Her mother wouldn't let her wear black. She said it was too slutty. Brown was okay so Ginny had found a kind of Maybelline, 2 for 99 cents, called Dark Brown that looked black. Her mother was too stupid to see through that one.

It was actually embarrassing how stupid her mother was, but sometimes it came in handy.

Gloss, eyeliner, and peach blush. Aces. *Judges say 9.5, 9.7, 9.9, 9.9 and 10! Average score 9.8. Crowd roars.* Everything had to be right and then no one could get you.

At the ugly kitchen table her mother stood over a plate of scrambled eggs and gross whole-wheat toast with her arms crossed, waiting. Ginny cruised by, grabbed her Lunchables from the counter and was heading for the hall when the usual tirade started up.

—Ginny you are not leaving this house without eating. I will not have you getting that anorexia thing just because the other girls do it!

—I already put my gloss on.

She had reached the front door.

—Dammit I'm fuckin late Riva, said her father, hustling through the kitchen with his jacket half on. —Gimme a new roll of Velamints, I ran out.

—Only have Certs, said her mother, opening a drawer. He was already grabbing for his cordless shaver that he used in the car.

—Batteries Riva, batteries, he said. She handed those over too. —What is this I said Duracell, always Duracell.

—They were on sale.

—It has to be Duracell. Outta here, and he walked past Ginny with a gross pat to her butt.

—Ginny I forbid you to go out that door without breakfast!

—The circumference of your eyeball is about 2π times .85 inches that is π times 4.318 centimeters which is approximately 13.5654 centimeters, flung Ginny, and slammed the door behind her. Free at last like that guy Martin Luther.

8:23

Alice opened a wary eye and stared across the blurry hill of pillow. The biker was still snoring. She could see every nick and pock in his weathered skin, and a scar arcing down from the corner of his eye to his earlobe.

He was not attractive. But then again, who was?

She rose carefully, not to ripple the mattress and alert him. But his heavy arm flopped off her as she rolled away, and he groaned.

Her left shoe lay tipped over on the carpet; she pulled it on and wriggled into her dress. Underwear was crumpled on a pile of *Skin & Ink* magazines, but on inspection turned out not to be hers. She flicked it away. She was scrabbling around in dirty laundry when the man stirred again.

—Hey. Wanna do it again?

—I'm sorry, said Alice. —I don't remember your name.

—Neither do I.

—If you remember mine I'm in the book.

He subsided with a grunt-sigh into the faded sheets. His hair was matted; his face was collapsed inward like a deflated football.

She found a single clean white shirt on a hanger in the closet and buttoned it over her dress.

—Borrowing your shirt, okay?

Above the basin of the bathroom sink, where green daubs of toothpaste formed a topography fuzzed with the scum of antique shaves, she splashed cold water on her face, combed her hair with her fingers, and rinsed her mouth under the tap. Cleaner but without underwear she strode through the naugahyde living room, past a three-foot bong filled with dirty water and an old black-velveteen poster of Kiss. She was reaching for the deadbolt when a voice made her jump.

—Just chew me up and spit me out. You bitch.

—Excuse me?

—You bitch. You're all the same.

Jack the Sailor was perched on a swing in his brass cage. She stood on tiptoe to look in: the cleanest space in the apartment. The bars gleamed, the feeder was fresh.

—You're a rude bird.

She turned away to open the door.

—Does a bear shit in the woods?

She closed the door behind her and scanned the street for her car. Dammit: they had left the bar on his Yamaha. She remembered. The parrot sat on his shoulder as they ran a red light, feathers ruffled by wind. There were cigar burns on his thighs; his tongue and mouth were Kools and Jägermeister. The wages of sin was the morning after.

But was it that bad? At least she'd watched the lights behind her blur, forgotten all giddiness wasn't her own, her laughing wasn't all of them laughing. She could have been anyone, and anyone was her: bad history was gone, replaced by a boundless future. In the dark streets became rivers. Tenements were mountains and the sky was a sea. Euphoria, brought to you by vermouth.

It was over now. By day the city was sharp, gray and light, a grid of obligation. She thumbed through the bills in her wallet: three dollars. She would have to take the bus straight to work, without going home. It wasn't the first time.

8:48

Decetes saw the sow from next door wallowing in her shrubbery, flapping a trotter in the wind as the hubby sped off in his dealmobile. They were the peasants of the postindustrial age. In feudal times those same vacant, bovine eyes had graced the faces of midwives and dung-sweepers.

—Bucella, Bucella, let down your golden hair! Oh Bucella! Bu-cel-la!

—Be quiet, some people are trying to sleep, scolded the midwife.

In feudal times she had loaned out her daughter to swineherds for a handful of copper. Those were the days.

—Not your daughter. She got it up bright and early. Bucella! Little pig little pig let me come in! I'll huff and I'll puff and I'll blow your house in!

—Don't even say my daughter's name, you molester. Just shut your filthy mouth.

—It is clean saints be praised. My sister cleaned it out with Borax a few minutes ago, or was it prussic acid. Bucella! By the hair of your chinny chin chin!

—I told you, be quiet! I'll have you arrested for disturbing the peace!

—If I may offer counsel on the subject of fashion, velour is not the fabric for your complexion nor is peach your best color. It sets off only the blackheads and other dermatological blemishes. I know. I am large-pored myself. It is a handicap, but not debilitating. Bucella! Bu-cel-la.

—I have never been spoken to—

—There is a first time for everything. Your finest hour has arrived. I, Dean Decetes, have spoken to you. I have bestowed upon you the remarkable gift of language. Use it wisely. Bu-cella!

—I have never!—

—I am not surprised, for I have seen your husband. He rides off in the morning to help his fellow tribesmen make their paintings on the wall of the cave. My good woman do not hold your breath, for it will be thousands of years before he stops his hunting-gathering to practice cultivation, and only then will the rudimentary signs of logos appear. In the beginning was the word, but before that there were beings like your husband. Bu-cella!

—Darn you! Be quiet Dean, shrieked Bucella, poking her head out the front door. —I hardly slept and now this.

—You will cut off these shackles or I will bellow till the walls cave in.

— Good morning Mrs. Frenter. All right Dean, I will cut them off, just be quiet. Come inside Dean. I mean now.

—Good night sweet lady, said Dean, —and remember what I said about the blackheads.

9:18

Alice stood near the back of the bus, hemmed in. It was crowded; she was breathing sweat disguised with pine-scent Mennen Speed Stick. An old man with a prosthetic foot hummed and nodded, a Latina in a nurse's uniform sat reading *Soap Opera Digest* across the aisle, and beside her a homeless woman in stained purple slacks stroked a wig in a plastic bag. Slumped down at the end of the back row, a skinny teenager with a pencil-thin moustache was crayoning stylized letters on the window beside him. *I tucked?* Probably not.

Unless it was a lullaby. *I tucked you in.*

Mornings like this almost made her suspect she was not upwardly mobile. *We're all so ugly, poor things.* She felt mute and claustrophobic and at the same time barely present, as though, by knowing she was ugly, she got to be outside looking in. By knowing her own grubby failure, she could take her judges by their shoulders and look at them squarely; she could say, *I know it, see? So I beat the rap.*

If there was another world, a better country. Elsewhere, away, the same people might be gathered: the same souls but transfigured. The planes of their cheeks were not dull with fatigue. They raced and spun and spread their arms. There was fresh air and there were prairies, forests. Towns where you walked on cobblestone streets, and music.

Alice felt tears on her cheeks. Dreams of running: the torture of the legless. She was still on the bus: they were all on the bus. They would always be on the bus, on their way to production. If anyone noticed her crying she would be embarrassed. She wiped the tears with the back of her fingers, felt her dry knuckles scrape. Dreams why not. Dreams why not? *I am lost. I am lost.*

Then she looked at the scribble on the window again. *I tucked you're sister.* There went the lullaby.

A warm meaty object settled on her skirt. Someone's hand.

—Get your hand off my ass, she hissed, and turned around to several faces, two men and a woman. The hand beat a hasty retreat: impossible to assign blame. They were a tightly packed throng, shoulders boxed.

—Get your hand offa my ass, jeered the graffiti artist. No one laughed.

—Shut up, said Alice.

—You shut up bitch. Shut your mouth bitch. Okay?

—What do you know about anything, you ignorant little shit. You're barely out of puberty and you go around defacing public property like this cesspool of a city doesn't have more to worry about than your stupid obscenities.

—Fuck you up lady, said the teen, thinning his lips out to expose a gold tooth.

—So do it, said Alice. —What do I have to live for. People like you?

—Let's all just calm down, said a man in a gray suit. He was the Speed Stick. —No violence please.

—Lady I fuck you up, said the tagger, and removed from his pocket in one graceful motion a battered knife. The old man with the prosthesis reached up and pulled the cord.

—Driver help, shrilled the nurse. —A man has a knife back here! Stop the bus!

—Please, said the gray suit, —no violence. We all have families. We're going to work!

The bus lurched to a halt, and passengers fell like dominos. Alice was pinned beneath a bearded man with halitosis, who turned and breathed into her face. The moist hand burrowed between her thighs. She kicked in panic and scrambled to her feet, scratching her leg, stepping on a fanned-out pool of black hair. The back doors opened and she was out, running, soles smacking the concrete, buildings moving up and down, eyes watering.

9:27

—I told you never to speak to the neighbors, said Bucella, pushing him down the stairs in front of her.

—Bucella my wrists were bleeding, chafed right through to the artery here. Another minute it would have been spurting like a geyser, I'd be shuffling off the mortal coil. It was life or death. Desperate measures. A man in pain does not think straight. It was not very Christian of you, Bucella, to make me wear the cuffs all night.

—Let the punishment fit the crime, said Bucella. —Put your hands on the edge of the workbench. And keep still.

—Yes Bucella.

The roar of the chainsaw filled their ears. Decetes could stomach many brands of atrocity, but the sharp teeth whirring near his fragile epidermis, the delicate digits with their complex network of veins and capillaries, their nerves and bone beneath the pristine surface so easily punctured by even the microscopic proboscis of a mosquito, impelled him to squeeze his eyes shut. He could feel the heat of the saw, the dust of friction, yes any minute he would be handless, plumes of blood like red ribbons would spring from his wrists, he would stagger as the crimson festooned the ceiling and floor, he would trip and dance, he would spray-paint inadvertently as his arms flopped, writing on the wall in blood, as his life's flow left him, the famous last words *Go home Dad your drunk.*

9:39

—Alice, said Phil Kreuz, startled as she burst into the office, panting and sweating from her run. His white forehead was looming. —You are in disrepair.

She dropped her bag on the carpet and looked down to see her black dress hiked up around her hips. The shirt hung down, but it was close. No underwear. She pulled the dress down. Under the glare of fluorescent wattage, modesty had been compromised.

Phil Kreuz was clearly mortified. He turned away and cleared his throat, making for the watercooler. She grabbed a tissue and wiped her face, stinging from air against tears. What stung: humiliation?

—Sorry, she said. —Kid pulled a knife on me in the bus. I got out the back and ran the whole way.

She walked over to her desk. *Erase yourself Alice. This is work.* Her legs still trembled. Sitting down hard she felt scared suddenly. Hadn't been before. Her pulse was racing. She took a deep breath, thought about putting her head between her legs. *It's fine now.* She should learn to keep her mouth shut. It would not be a dignified death.

—It is a mistake for a female to board a rapid transit vehicle, said Phil. —In my view it constitutes an act of negligence. I advise against it. Under no circumstances would I permit Barbara to place herself in that situation.

—I know Phil, see my problem is I don't have a husband like you to tell me what to do so I'm pretty much at the mercy of chance.

—An informed choice can always be made, said Phil, filling his paper cone to the brim, then cutting off the flow at the critical moment so that a shimmering meniscus curved above the rim. He raised the cone carefully without spilling a drop, then tipped it into his mouth.

Alice harbored a phobic loathing of his wiry brown handlebar mustache. She looked away as he drank. It was early. They were alone in the office. She sat back in her chair, took another deep breath and stretched out her legs. Her feet were sore from high-impact contact in the tight shoes. It was a relief to know she was a wreck, a waste. It lightened the burden. There was no need for achievement. She slipped the shoes off and stretched them, splaying her toes in the air.

—I believe—hygiene regulations? began Phil Kreuz. He was a by-the-book man. Clinically there was a possibility he was obsessive compulsive, but she was not qualified to diagnose.

—Phil, I just ran six blocks in these shoes, she said. —I respect your professionalism but please have a heart. There's no one else here. I promise, I'm not a carrier of athlete's foot, plantar warts or hoof and mouth disease.

—Foot and mouth, corrected Phil Kreuz. —Commonly associated with cattle.

—There you go.

He cleared his throat again, caressed his mustache and walked, with stiff military gait, to a potted philodendron against the wall. He inspected a leaf. She extracted a black comb from her bag and ran it through her hair.

—Where is your four-door Mazda, said Phil Kreuz, turning from the philodendron.

—Um, it's in the shop, said Alice. —The, uh, CV boots disintegrated.

—Most accredited auto shops provide dropoff services for their customers, said Phil Kreuz, nodding to himself. His eyes flicked nervously from her toes to her shoes. —Dealerships certainly.

—If only you had told me that before, Phil, said Alice. —It would have saved me all this trauma.

—Barbara was in a fire last night, he revealed abruptly.

It was a rare personal disclosure.

—Oh, said Alice. —A big one?

—Two fire trucks, said Phil Kreuz. —A residential fire. She is unharmed.

—I'm glad to hear that, said Alice. —What a relief for you.

—Of course I should not have permitted her to attend, said Phil Kreuz, shaking his head. —A social gathering with alcohol. Inappropriate. I should not have allowed her to go. She is unharmed, but in a state of shock.

—Well, Phil, said Alice, slipping her left foot back into its shoe, —sometimes a person needs to get out. Don't blame yourself Phil. It's not your fault. A fire is force majeure. An act of God Phil, so to speak. Beyond your control.

—In the first place, she should not have been permitted to attend such a gathering, said Phil Kreuz, pacing, fondling the mustache. —Alcohol, and a large number of guests. She should have been with me at the Reading Room. We had a discussion group.

Phil had recently been forced to miss a Church of Christ Scientist meeting for a funeral. Alice remembered his reluctance.

—Sunday evening discussion group, he ruminated. —She did not wish to attend. It was her sister's birthday.

—You did the right thing Phil, said Alice. —Don't blame yourself.

She stood and lifted the coffee pot from the corner of her desk.

—Blood, said Phil Kreuz.

—Pardon me?

—Blood, he repeated, and pointed, eyes bulging, at the back of her leg. She twisted and looked down. A long drip was approaching her ankle from a scratch on the back of her thigh.

—Flesh wound Phil, nothing more. From the bus.

—Antiseptic wipes at the First Aid station, said Phil. —Hydrogen Peroxide, U.S.P. 3% Topical Anti-Infective. Do not move. It could get onto the floor. I will bring you a swab.

Bucella came in while Alice was standing beside her desk awaiting his return. —I don't get it, said Alice. —Aren't they supposed to not believe in medicine, or something? The Christian Scientists?

—I don't know.

—I saw your brother at a party last night, by the way.

—You have my condolences, said Bucella.

—He did not wish to attend an AA meeting, said Alice.

—I am not surprised, said Bucella. —Your leg is bleeding.

—Nothing, a scrape. Phil's getting me something for it. He fell on top of me and had an erection.

—My Lord, said Bucella, white-faced.

—He said it was his lighter.

—But Phil doesn't smoke!

—Your brother, Bucella. Phil doesn't get erections.

—Shh!

—Three swabs, said Phil. —Dispose of them by placing them in this Ziploc bag, then sealing it. A receptacle in the ladies' room would be best.

—Thank you Phil. I appreciate it. Phil's wife was in a fire last night.

—Lord, said Bucella.

—She is physically unharmed, said Phil, tight-lipped, and turned his back.

—I apologize for my brother.

—You are not your brother's keeper Bucella, lighten up. Anyway Bucella, I have strayed from the fold. I'm not exactly a walking advertisement for the Twelve Steps.

—The path is not an easy one, I understand, said Bucella, from behind her partition. Alice heard the hum of her computer.

—What happened to you?

Finally, a secular presence.

—Cut myself.

—Rusty blade? That's a beautiful dress.

—It stinks of cigarettes and beer.

—You smell like a rose garden. Good morning Bucella.

—Ernest—

—I downloaded new sample data to your folder, Phil Kreuz told Ernie, wiping his fingers with a moist towelette as he passed. —For the radon dose-response model. From Utica.

—Thank you Phillip, said Ernie, and winked at Alice.

10:10

He had seen it. Blond hairs. Bermuda Triangle. The, within. No, no. Banish. *Sins of the body are a concession to brute matter and deny His sovereignty. God works in the spirit. The physical dimensions of our lives are creations of our limited perception. Matter is a distortion of the senses. Everything from lust to subtle acedia.*

Still, she needed his help, she sought his guidance, she was lost without him, a golden virgin. But home is where the heart is. And so careless. He could shield her if only she asked. He had been fully prepared to apply the swabs himself. Closer to the source, he might have seen again. Kneeling. Touching. Then—interruptus! Intruders. Heat filled his cheeks. It was shameful. Self-control! Discipline.

Phillip retired to his cubicle, where he sprayed the desktop, as per usual, with disinfectant. It was a necessary precaution due to the unsanitary habits of the so-called sanitation workers who were charged with the task of cleaning the workstations at the end of the day. They were not trustworthy. He had recently observed a hispanic housekeeping employee, bearing the nametag *Jesus* on the breast pocket of his blue uniform, crunching his cigarette butt into the soil of a ficus tree. The premises were nonsmoking, of course.

He had reported the transgression of this apocryphal Jesus to Ernest, but strongly suspected he had taken no action. Ernest routinely ignored memoranda pertaining to the problems Phillip documented. He put them in the Circular File. This, at least, was Phillip's strong intuition. Ernest did not take hygiene seriously. Cavalier attitudes like his were the fuel that powered diseases in the Third World, the oil that greased the wheels of raging superviruses. They were directly responsible for the flies in the eyes of African children, the sores on beggars in Calcutta. Without cleanliness there could be no godliness, and vice versa. Dirt begat death.

Ernest had had the temerity to rebuke him for spraying his keyboard, on the grounds that the liquid could seep between the keypads and disturb their operation. Phillip remembered the incident clearly. Ernest had leaned over his shoulder and asked him what he was doing. —Better leave that to the folks who deal with the hardware, Phillip, he had said.

—The numbers from Utica, he said now, over the partition. —You remember offhand what the sample size was?

The informality of Ernest was seldom refreshing.

—It is in the file, said Phillip coldly.

Ernest moved away, nearly colliding with an approaching Bucella as Phillip gritted his teeth.

—Oh—excuse me Ernest! said Bucella. —Phillip, will you still be able to bring Barbara for dinner tonight? After her traumatic experience?

—I believe so, said Phillip, nodding. —It is scheduled. I am sure her morale will be restored by this evening. She was physically unharmed.

—Oh good, said Bucella. —I'll make spinach lasagna.

Phillip did not favor Italian fare.

—We will be punctual.

She was a devout woman in her way, but Catholics were notoriously flighty. They were given to weeping and gruesome depictions of the Crucifixion. Moreover they were often lower-class immigrants with a dark and promiscuous attitude toward sins of the flesh. Also they were quite melodramatic, a definite sign of incipient mental illness. It was from their parent country that the fat women singing piercingly came, and the men blown up like bullfrogs.

Many of these puffed-up singing men merely pretended to be Catholics, but were in truth deviants. You could tell just by looking at them. Such men were more than unpleasant, they were a threat to public morals. Barbara had tried to watch *The Three Tenors* on public television just two weeks previously, forcing Phillip to confiscate the remote control. He had set her straight on the subject of these three so-called tenors, deviants one and all. He would not be surprised if the one with the beard soiled innocent children on a regular basis. He was too fruity even for the other Sodomites. Phillip had written a series of letters to PBS regarding *The Three Tenors* but had received, as yet, no reply. In addition, many non-Sodomites, poor people with dangerous hygiene habits, were, in addition, Catholics. An ominous connection.

He had also been forced to take disciplinary action when Barbara attempted to watch a narrative drama entitled *Murder She Wrote*, a virtual Gomorrah of prime-time indecency in which females far past their prime rudely rejected appropriate modes of behavior and seldom if ever acknowledged their spiritual debt to the savior. Failing, in that unseemly instance, to gain possession of the remote, he had gone straight for the fusebox. Nipped it in the bud.

However, Bucella Decetes demonstrated remarkable restraint, for a Catholic. At least she was polite and neat, unlike some other employees of Statistical Diagnostics he could name.

10:28

Her knees were shaking. It was from the nearness of Ernest. In her cubicle she stared at a Garfield card sent to her by an aunt in Anaheim and tacked to her bulletin board. There was nothing funny about a cat with a stupid face.

Beside Garfield was a postcard of a place called Chichén Itzá in Mexico. It had not been sent to her but to Alice Reeve, but Alice Reeve had thrown it out. Bucella had never been to *Chichén Itzá Historic Site of Ancient Mayan Temple*, but there was something about it. Men with painted chests and long black hair beat drums and chanted. Carried aloft on a flowery bier was a young, beautiful Maiden, clad in white. She had long hair and clear skin. It did not look like Bucella, but it was her.

The skirt of her flowing dress hung down on each side of the bier, flowing. The strong men danced, they beat the ground with ornamental sticks and howled. Jungle trees were a backdrop. Up the long stone ramp they carried her. Carvings of monsters flashed by. Women pulled out their hair, mothers wept. Little children tore their teeth out.

Black thunderclouds were low on the horizon, the air was moist and warm, and Bucella could smell incense. Pyres burned and columns of smoke like purple tornados rose into the orange sky. It was common knowledge that she was a Virgin. Her hair was beautiful. Her dress continued to flow. They were bearing her to the Well. They would drop her in from high above, from the roof of the Temple. They reached the summit and lowered the bier onto a marble platform. She was anointed with something. They bowed down before her. They raised their muscled arms to the sky and called upon the primitive rain god which was actually just a bunch of meteorological conditions.

Then came the High Priest in ceremonial robes, wearing a headdress of pure gold inlaid with big jewels. It was Ernest. They knelt at his tanned feet and chanted, urging him to hurl her to her sacrificial death. Ernest's eyes met hers. Her eyes also met his. He lifted her up high, preparing to drop her into the fiery Pit. Then, gently, he lowered her to her feet beside the Well. He turned to the populace teeming on the ground at the bottom of the temple. He raised his staff, at the end of which was a serpent's head with ruby eyes, that looked kind of Egyptian even though he was Mexican. His voice boomed out strong and determined. —No. I will not let her die.

The crowd was taken aback since they had been expecting a good sacrifice, but then a low murmur rushed through their ranks. They were in awe of the High Priest. He knew best. They prostrated themselves by the thousands crying with joy. —She shall be my sacred bride, said Ernest. —Okay, said the crowd in one Voice. Night began to fall as they were borne aloft to the bridal temple. The crowd rejoiced. The children's teeth were set back into their heads by fully qualified oral surgeons.

Or maybe they were baby teeth anyway. Yes. Baby teeth so the real teeth just grew in. It was fine.

She stopped looking at Chichén Itzá. It was just a pile of ruins anyway, where heathens had run around clubbing each other on the head. While good things came to those who waited and the Meek should inherit the Earth, it was true that Job, visited by Plagues and Pestilence, had not lived happily ever after. So far she was Job, in a more subtle way. She would have to make a leap of faith. A Leap was required for Salvation. She was called upon to throw Caution to the Winds. Ernest had to realize she was the One.

—Your brother called me a zealot and a missionary, said Alice, craning her neck around the partition.

—That's nice, said Bucella. There was no privacy here. Laws of Personal Space were not respected. Bucella picked up a sheet of paper and a pen, concealed it in the pocket of her denim skirt and padded across the carpet to the restroom. She locked herself into a toilet stall, sat down and began to write.

When souls are twinned they should not be divided. They should cleave unto each other. We are trapped in our earthly Bodies, these mundane Forms, we have to bring them together & dance a holy Dance, the dance of Life itself while He looks on smiling above us. Love is God's gift. At the end of all things it will be you & I. In Kingdom Come we will stand together beneath the invisible door with Garlands on our heads

—Is that you Bucella? I'd know those wedge heels anywhere. I'm out of TP, could you pass me a couple of squares?

garlands of flowers. We will stand on the helm of the great Ship of the everlasting Life. We will be together in Love, Glory &

—You're still in here? I happen to know through no fault of my own that Phil Kreuz is hoarding Ex Lax in his desk drawer, want me to get some for you?

Glory & eternal Union.

She folded it carefully, flushed in case Alice was still in proximity, slid it into her pocket and emerged from the stall to the vacant bay of sinks. She would put it on his desk, unsigned, after hours. At Statistical Diagnostics everything was electronic. He did not know her handwriting. So he would only know the letter was written by her if he already understood her and loved her too. Green valleys misty clouds!

She returned to her cubicle with trembling hands and dialed her home number.

—Pick up if you're there Dean. I need to talk to you. I'm having a coworker and his wife over for dinner at seven and you better not be there. You hear me Dean? You can come home after midnight. I meant to discuss it this morning but I got distracted by that little accident. Don't embarrass me Dean or I'll kick you out for good.

11:19

—You bitch Bucella, said Decetes to the answering machine.
—You did it on purpose.

He had wrapped an old shirt around the wounded fingers. It was not his fault he had fainted: the noise had proved overwhelming. He would exact his revenge.

But first he would visit the magazine office for a brief talk with the indentured editorial servants. HQ was located, conveniently, beside a bar. Sadly the Pinto was parked on a high-income avenue in Santa Monica, or possibly corralled in a police impound lot under lock and key. The transportation infrastructure was failing, and the blame for this lamentable circumstance lay, like so many tragedies of state, on his sister. Fortunately he held her Visa Debit card in the palm of his unmaimed hand, sweaty but secure.

He left the front door unlocked, as per usual, and walked to the automatic teller machine on the corner, where he swiftly and efficiently removed $100. While the taxi driver played Tex-Mex music on his crappy radio Decetes stealthily appropriated a racing form from under the passenger seat, though he was uncertain it would prove germane to his day's undertakings.

Passing the receptionist in the lobby, he broke wind with quiet grace. She had slighted him once, and he was not a man to forgive and forget. In the employee lunchroom, which housed a microwave encrusted with ossified Lean Cuisine remnants, he lingered to browse through the refrigerator. He was just getting a grip on someone's ham sandwich when a square-faced German woman from Personnel tapped his shoulder.

—Stealink again? she asked sternly.

—I do not steal, said Decetes firmly. —I merely take what is mine.

She stared at him malevolently.

—And everything is mine.

He would deal with her later.

—Yesterday, said Alan H. calmly when Decetes entered his office. A trollop stood next to his desk, her thin bootheels wobbling as she adjusted the strap on her purse.

—Hey ho, up she rises, said Decetes with jovial mien, but Alan H. shook his head. He was having none of it.

—Yesterday was your deadline Decetes, said Alan H. —You missed it again.

—What is time, said Decetes, bowing in the strumpet's direction. She was pulling at the zipper on her fake alligator boots, leaning down so that the orbs of flesh, easily 46 D Decetes would claim if it came to a wager, hung like sallow fruit. —Madam, is time a commodity? Is time a square with equal sides, a block of base metal to be welded to a grid of little lives and weigh there till the lives come to an end? Or is time the river Yangtze, the Ganges or the Nile, with her headwaters in Shangri La and her mouth in Babylon?

—Shut up Decetes, said Alan H. He was a Philistine, lacking the poet's ear for epic phraseology. —Time is your ass Decetes. You don't have those reviews for me in two hours, I'll write 'em myself and you're out of here. I have plenty of slimy freelancers Decetes. I have guys who will write those things for nothing but the free tapes. And I'm tired of your crap. It's not like it takes talent.

—The point is made, rest assured, said Decetes smoothly. Alan H. was of the old school when it came to human resource management: he would have felt quite at home lashing apple-cheeked toddlers in a coal mine. —I am almost finished with my work.

—Work, yeah, said Alan H. —Your work. Go do it Decetes.

—Alan, I'll see you at the photoshoot okay? said the porn slut. —I gotta go to the bathroom.

—I am going that way myself, said Decetes. —Let me escort you out. I will keep the wolves from your door.

CHAPTER THE THIRD

Strife rears its head; Lust makes an appearance;
and a Prince among men is repeatedly battered

—She is not at home, said Phil Kreuz. He was pacing agitatedly, chafing his hairy white wrists. Alice crumpled the Saran Wrap from her sprout sandwich and lobbed it into the wastebasket, narrowly missing his polycotton pantleg. —She assured me she would have a Meditation Day.

—Maybe she's asleep Phil. Or, uh, meditating at the Reading Room or shopping. You worry too much.

—I am taking half a sick day, said Phil Kreuz. —I will advise Personnel.

—Get some rest Phil. You seem tenser than usual.

—Replace it regularly. Bacteria accumulates between the abrasion and the absorbent pad.

—What?

—The Bandaid.

—Thanks Phil. But listen, can I ask you a personal question?

—It, I think—

—It's about the doctrine, you know the whole, like the idea of your faith, isn't there something in there about mind over matter or something? Physical things not being real, or something? Where you're not allowed to go to the Emergency Room if you're sick?

—Of course Alice, that is—

—So all this, the issue of hygiene—

—Hygiene is not medicine.

—But uh. . . .

—It is commonly known that public transportation is utilized by vagrants and perpetrators of violent crime during the evening hours. Females are at high risk.

—Okay Phil. I appreciate your concern.

He strode out nodding. Alice slipped her shoes off again, put her feet up on the desk and started to clip her fingernails.

—Alice darling, how brazen, said Ernie, coming up behind her. —We fags can't get away with that. Nail clipping in broad daylight! So earthy. Only a Barbie doll like you could pull it off. Do you have an emery board?

—Top drawer on the left, said Alice.

He pulled the drawer open and extracted her nail file.

—There's a show tonight if you want to come, he said. —I would love to see you. I could introduce you to Jerome.

—I have to go to a stupid bachelorette party.

—I'm wearing that vintage crinoline, he said, filing. —I'd like to know what you think.

—I'll try to get away early.

—Excuse me, um Ernest?

He stopped filing. —Yes Bucella, may I help you?

—I was wondering, she said, clasping her hands together, —I'm having Phil and Babs Kreuz over for dinner tonight and I wanted to see if you could, uh—invite you too. Oh and you too Alice. It's just lasagna.

—How thoughtful! said Ernie. —It's just Alice and I were just saying, we have a prior engagement tonight. May I take a raincheck?

—Oh, said Bucella. —Oh yes. Maybe next week?

—Babs? said Alice. —That's his wife? Where've I heard that lately?

—Barbara, said Bucella. —Babs for short.

—Oh my! Better get back to work, said Ernie, and was through his office door before Bucella could cash in her check.

Bucella lingered there, standing awkwardly, and readjusted her reading glasses on the bridge of her nose.

—Does he, does Ernest have a girlfriend?

The closet door stood wide open, but Bucella only banged her head against the jamb.

—A girlfriend, no Bucella. He does not.

12:21

Bucella turned away, relieved. There was nothing between them. He only talked to Alice out of Charity. Jesus healed the Lepers.

12:50

She was taking forever in the bathroom. Decetes had trotted out a quotation from Coleridge, though the trollop didn't know Coleridge from a hole in the wall. A good thing too since Decetes had probably misquoted. —In Xanadu did Kubla Khan a stately pleasure dome decree, where Alph the sacred river ran through caverns measureless to man down to a sunless sea, he had said at the door to the ladies' room.

She shut it in his face, as though to warn him coyly from the feminine domain. It was a saucy maneuver. And yes, he had subsequently made a rapid break for the men's, but had returned in short order. It was widely known that women's urinary tracts were sluggish; surely she could not have beat him to the punch?

But she was not emerging.

The Kraut with the shelf bosom passed him frowning as he made his way to the kitchen. He still had a score to settle with her. At the timeclock he paused to locate her timecard, on the corner of which, with fastidious care, he placed a tiny gift from his nose. Let the punishment fit the crime.

It was dirty work, but it had to be done.

He pushed the ladies' room door open a crack, checking one last time. —You in there? he called, but was pushed out of the way by a pinch-faced slattern from Production.

In the lobby downstairs he waited fifteen minutes, but the trollop made no appearance. Possibly she had decamped by way of the parking garage. Well, even female dogs were reluctant to mate; for this reason male dogs were fitted out with a penis head which, when erect and inserted, blossomed out into a barbed mushroom and thereby locked itself into the feminine orifice, preventing escape. Belly to back the dogs cavorted in a yard or basement, the female yelping with pain and annoyance.

Now for a drink. He was $90 in the black. Later he might seek his fortune at Santa Anita.

The alcohol emporium was deserted; sun not quite over the yardarm, perhaps. He took his place at the counter and ordered a whiskey from the sagging barmaid. She wore a ring in her nose and a rose tattoo on her upper arm. Disenfranchised youth had a penchant for scarification: too confused to target their oppressors, they chose themselves as victims. They perpetrated impotent violence against their own sorry meat. Decetes raised his glass.

—What's your name? he asked.

—Dani, she said, swabbing the bar with a greasy white rag.

—I drink to your tattoo Dani. Dani does the rose symbolize purity, or have you been deflowered?

—Watch your mouth or you won't get served, buddy.

—No Dani, no. You are wrong. There are millions who serve me. My name is Alpha and Omega. My name is Krishna, Jehovah and Zeus.

—That so.

—I am as small as the quark, Dani, and as large as the universe, ever-expanding. I am steady-state and Big Bang.

—You won't be banging in here.

—Dani I have been known to pollinate little flowers, the common along with the rare. I dip my pistil in the stamen and new life sprouts forth. My seeds are germinating everywhere Dani. Roses are among my favorites. Dani, you can be in my herbaceous border.

—Forget it. One more drink and you're out.

—Then make it a triple.

—Jim, Ryan! Meet Alfie Nomega. He says he's a Hare Krishna.

—Where's your orange dress man?

—Begone Jim, begone Ryan, said Decetes, lifting his glass. —We would be alone. Have you considered nude modeling, Dani?

—Barbara? Barbara! called Phillip, entering the living room. He flicked the front door locked behind him. Then, quite suddenly, he apprehended the presence of a large mechanical bull.

—Not at work? she asked, emerging from the kitchen. She was garbed in a floral brassiere and panties, and her white skin shone with lubricant. It was a disturbing sight; surely something was wrong in the world. Yes: this was wrong. By no means was it right.

Phillip dropped his briefcase, closed his eyes and counted slowly to ten, inhaling and exhaling carefully.

—I require answers to the following two questions, he said when he had regained his composure. —One: why is that distasteful object in our home. Two: why are you walking around in undergarments with oil on your person. You will answer these questions slowly and succinctly.

—For exercise. Mail-order merchandise.

He cocked his head to one side and raised an eyebrow, waiting. His great aunt Gloria had said at church once that he was "patrician." He recalled clearly: he had been 12 years old at the time, and had worn a blue suit. She was dead of emphysema but he had not forgotten. In times of crisis, the word *patrician* perched on his shoulders like two great eagles.

—This is tanning gel. Self-tanning. It doesn't work right away though. It takes—

—One, said Phillip with deliberation. —A mechanical bull has been purchased. I see on the box, Bronco Bill is the name of the item. Two, you have covered your seminude body in a cosmetics product. Barbara, one plus two makes covetousness and vanity. One plus two makes Barbara a sinner and a worshipper of lust.

—But I just want to get rid of some flab!

—Barbara needs to work harder. Repeat after me. The material world is a human creation. God works in the Spirit. Vanity is a concession to the brute matter of a spiritually debased world.

—But I just want to get rid of some flab!

—I am satisfied with your corporeal shell, and I am your husband. Remember: the flesh is a rotten vessel. Now repeat what I said.

—Bronco Bill is good for abs, she said, trotting back into the kitchen to rip a paper towel off the roll. He stood his ground, arms akimbo. —Better than Stairmaster, plus lots of excitement in your own home.

—We will be returning it to the manufacturers first thing tomorrow morning, said Phillip, and sat down on the couch.

—I don't want to return it! said Barbara, patting oil off her chest. —I'm keeping it! I'll put it in my Personal Room. I paid with my own money. From Daddy.

—Changes of environment must be consentual. No elements disagreeable to either party are permitted to enter the apartment. It is in our prenuptial contract.

—You never consent, and but I *always* do. I get to keep Bronco Bill. I get to keep him keep him keep him. *Science and Health* doesn't say you can't buy Bronco Bill.

—No Barbara. But when Mary Baker Eddy wrote *Science and Health* there were no Bronco Bills.

—I want to be the best possible me.

—The subject is closed Barbara. Before our dinner engagement you will accompany me to the Reading Room and study the mind of Christ.

—Restrain yourselves, said Decetes, retreating. —I meant no disrespect, my good men. Amateur pornography would be the ideal venue for Dani. Showcase her attributes.

—You don't know when to shut up, said Ryan the Bouncer, and Decetes fell back onto a table, crunching a wet glass beneath his kidney. Inferior workmanship was so often the norm. The glassblowers of Venice would weep.

Ryan had knobby forearms, and his knuckles were red.

—Don't hurt me, begged Decetes. He could be flexible. —I'm Neil Bush. I'm the President's brother. Savings and loan, ring any bells? The Secret Service has their day off but repercussions may be stringent. Look at my hands! Injured by investors, foaming at the mouth. I was defending our free nation!

—I'm gonna beat your face in. You were talking to my wife back there, said Ryan. —You got balls Hare Krishna? Let's see.

2:23

Ginny was getting ready to pass a note to Mike Lamota when the lights went on all of a sudden and everyone had to wake up. At the back Liza B. and Ricky were making out under the counter with the Bunsen burner on it like they always did in Biology videos and Ginny saw Ricky bang his head as he got up.

—Who turned the lights on? said Mr. Damofrio, mad.

Then Ginny's stomach flopped. Her mother was *actually standing* at the classroom door in her orange dressing gown with egg down the front and the rabbit slippers! Ginny scrambled off her stool and knelt beneath the counter out of sight. Gross. It smelled like sulfur. The rotten-egg gas.

—Are you the one? shrilled her mother.

Oh no, oh no no no. Cube root 63, 3.97905, cube root 192, 5.76899, cube root 1226, 10.70278.

She was yelling at Mr. Damofrio. —Are you the one? Filling my daughter's head with those filthy ideas? I found this in her room this morning! It's a diaphragm! I found the box it came in!

Ginny heard them all whispering and laughing. She looked out from beneath the counter and saw her mother throw it on the floor. *No way. No way no way no way.*

—Gross! said Liza B., and Mike Lamota was laughing his head off with Ricky and Michael D. —Wack!

—Mrs.—, uh we should talk about this outside, said Mr. Damofrio in a hurry. *Cube root 775, 9.18545.*

—No! I want these young people to know! Ginny? Are you in here? yelled her mother. Ginny stayed where she was, looking sideways at Michael D. who rolled his eyes. —This school is run by perverts! Sex perverts! I want my daughter back! Because of you people and your perverted sex education she is having relations! She is thirteen years old! She is a mathematics gifted with her whole life ahead of her, and she is having relations! Teenage pregnancies! Abortions!

—Mrs.—? No one has counseled your daughter to have an abortion, I promise you. If—

—Ginny? Come talk to your mother! Where is she?

Ricky was pointing. She couldn't believe it. He was pointing at her where she hid. She flipped him the bird. Pigface shitwad. No way. She had to get up before she was cornered. She rose and grabbed her teddybear knapsack.

—Ginny!

She had the bag over her shoulder. She dashed past Liza B. and Ricky, pushed her mother aside and was out the door, down the hall. Out the metal doors. Her mother's Honda hatchback was parked in the lot. The door was open and the key was in the ignition. She got in and jammed down the emergency brake.

—Ginny! shrieked her mother, behind her. —Wait for me!

3:41

—I'll pay you back tomorrow.

—I'm sure you will, said Bucella, and withdrew two crisp fives from her mauve vinyl wallet. Alice took them and crumpled them in her hand, hopping while she adjusted a shoe.

—It's a bachelorette party, we were all assigned gifts. I have to get a vibrator shaped like a banana but I don't have my car here and I can't face the bus again.

—I see, said Bucella. Flushed, she opened and closed a drawer to look preoccupied, then snapped the wallet closed and replaced it carefully in her purse.

—Personally I have no interest in bananas, I want you to know that right up front, said Alice, gathering up her pile of Band-Aids.

Alice was confusing. Sometimes she said Profanities, but other times she was almost quite nice.

—I'm sorry Bucella, this is an inappropriate subject. So Phil and Barbara are dining with you tonight?

—Yes they are. I'm hoping it will improve my work relationship with Phillip. He's so quiet. And he didn't come for Thanksgiving.

—I hear his wife has some kind of disorder.

—Disorder?—

—She's a little slow. Ernie met her once. Slow but steady, Bucella.

—Special people often have great faith in God, said Bucella.

—And well they might, said Alice. —Thanks for the loan.

4:04

Decetes had fetched up in a patch of scrub weed along the edge of a parking lot. They had chased him. The sharp end of a fallen brown palm frond was gouging his ear. On a rise in the nearby soil, he watched a beetle bury its black ass in the sand. A stinkbug, no doubt. Or perhaps a dung beetle. Sticky blood was caking over his eyelid. He raised his maimed hands, divested now of bandages, and waved them above his face to ensure he still had his vision. Yes. Five fingers on each hand. He counted ten in all. That seemed correct.

He was frequently the target of brute force. It was scarcely a surprise, for all true heroes were misunderstood by the rabble. The very underclass whose sensibilities he nobly championed turned upon him in blind wrath and battered him to a pulp. Like rabid dogs they bit the hand that fed.

Tentatively he adjusted the frond so that his head lay on its brittle leaves. The bushmen of the Kalahari slept flat on the sand but held their sleeping heads up off the ground: for they knew well what small and many-legged animals might infiltrate their ears in R.E.M. He would be wise to do the same.

Above him stretched the pale-blue sky with its hem of gray filth near terra firma, where the endless prairie of the stratosphere met Los Angeles city limits. Writ large over the banks of fleecy clouds, in so-far invisible ink, was his name.

He squinted and lifted a leg, testing his motor abilities. All was well, but he must rest awhile.

He was frequently beaten by men. Women, being weak of sinew, did not dare attack his cage of meat and brawn; but men often laid siege to the fortress of his body. Luckily their efforts were geared toward the short term. With men, he took the beating and then he recovered. He was permitted to relax between beatings. God bless the men, for they were simple brutes. With women the battle was gradual and wearing. It never let up; it was insidious and stealthy.

A wasp alighted on his arm and he watched its wings move as it crawled between a cut and a hair. Presently it rose and disappeared. Animals had superior justice. The wasp refused to sting a wounded man. Its peers, no doubt, had prevailed upon it to extract some resource from Decetes; but the wasp, having surveyed the damage, decided for charity and made itself scarce.

If only he could rally the wasps to his cause. There was a language barrier, sadly. Like it or not, the women and the men would be rolled beneath the wheel of progress some day soon, and that wheel was named Dean Decetes. Some would be crushed and others would be spared. These were the lucky few. Their names were already inscribed upon a roster somewhere, the roster of the faithful. The faithful would align themselves with him, a cadre of mighty lieutenants.

—How come you lyin' there, said a kid, looming above with a translucent green plastic submachine gun in hand.

It was a hispanic kid of the male gender. Spic spawn. Pope progeny.

—Begone Pedro, mumbled Decetes. —I would be alone.

—How you know my name, said the spawn.

—I am a God among men, murmured Decetes. —I am Jesus Christ crucified. Can't you tell kid? Take a look at my hands.

—You not Jesus gringo. Jesus he dead.

—Resurrected, don't you know the Bible Pedro?

—Jesus gots a beard.

—Shaved it off, you beaneater. You think I don't have access to a disposable Gillette? I told you I'm Jesus. Now run back to your hovel and get me a drink. A glass of water. Go!

—Jesus don't say swearwords.

—Chinga tu madre Pedro. A glass of water or you will be barred forever from the gates of heaven. I mean business Pedro.

—You stink Jesus.

—Here Pedro, here. See this? It's a one-dollar bill. You send this to Mexico City, your grandmother can buy herself a condo. Get me some water and I'll let you have it.

—Okay stinky Jesus, easy money. Wait here Jesus.

4:28

Ginny cruised slowly along her street in the Honda. Had to pick up her stuff at the house, but only if there was no one home. Her mother had to be in hysterics by now. She might even have called the police. Four lawns to go, three. Yep, there she was. Outside. She was still wearing her ugly robe.

But what was she doing? She was at the old lech's front door, her back turned. Her right arm moved. Omigod, she was spraying purple stuff on their door. She had flipped. Those dumb tapes from the family counselor had finally driven her up the wall. Once Ginny stole one and listened to it on her Walkman. It was weird and pathetic. *Visualize clear sparkling water and repeat: blame is not productive.*

Ginny sped up and drove past. Maybe she could sneak in and get her stuff at night, through the window. Find Lucas or Mitch and get them to boost her up. Plus she needed a place to crash. Liza B. hated her now like all the other girls. She was just jealous but it was sad anyway. Find some guy and go home with him, but no one from school. She couldn't face them. Never again. A titty bar maybe. Guys there were desperate.

She turned the car around and headed east.

5:02

Zamphir Flute played on Bucella's car stereo. She had bought it many years ago but it was still good to calm frazzled nerves. She stood on the threshold of an Epiphany. In the morning Ernest would find the note, albeit unsigned.

Pulling up the driveway, she saw something purple on her front door. Purple letters! She jumped out and left the car idling. Across the front door someone had painted two purple words. CHILD MOLESTER.

Tribulations! She was being Tested. And the Kreuzes were coming. Dean, as usual, had somehow brought Dishonor upon her house. Had he done something bad? She turned back to her car, but it was rolling backward into the street. No! Someone was driving. At the wheel was her next door neighbor.

—Stop! What are you doing? cried Bucella, and ran after the car, but the woman ignored her, reversing into the street, then pulling forward as Bucella pounded on the driver's side window. Her housekeys were in the ignition. —Stop! Mrs. Frenter?

5:57

It said GIRLS GIRLS GIRLS, just like in the movies, flashing red. Prime spot for desperate guys. She could doctor her mother's license for fake ID, change the date and put her own picture in. First she had to park the hatchback. It had embarrassing bumperstickers, BABY ON BOARD and I BRAKE FOR KITTYCATS. Wack. She was peeling the plastic off her old Arizona learner's permit to get the photo out when a sleazebag in acid-wash jeans tapped on the window.

—Baby you want a quick buck? Quick buck for quick fuck?

—Get out of my face. I got mace in the glove compartment.

—Oooh baby she talk dirty.

6:04

—$39.99 for a lousy vibrator, you have to be kidding me. Don't you have anything cheaper?

—We may have a smaller banana model for $31.99 if you prefer something modest.

—A yellow dildo marked CHIQUITO HAND-PICKED is modest? Don't you have sales on these things? Clearance on last-year's models?

—We are selling the Misses' Missile model at a mark-down. $19.99. It's a novelty item.

—Jesus Christ it says SCUD on the side.

6:12

A splinter of wood from the window frame was lodged in her thumb. Mrs. Frenter had gone crazy. It was not her fault.

Bucella had found paint in the basement after breaking in, but it was all dried up. The wreath she had made for Thanksgiving would have to serve her purpose. It was large, with orange ribbons, dried red corncobs, oak leaves and a pilgrim doll peeking out from behind a gourd. She hung it on the front door. Now only CHI and STER showed. In the dark, Phillip Kreuz and his wife might not notice.

After she called the police to report her car stolen, she put on Hildegarde of Bingen and began to layer mozzarella into the casserole.

6:29

Decetes had misjudged. The Spic spawn had returned with his brother, who had proved uncompromising on the subject of money. Decetes had been forced to yield up his savings, though not before the older Spic cut a swath of hair off his head. A premature bald spot, cuts on his wrists, a finger almost severed at the second knuckle, a sprained ankle and a black eye.

The ground was becoming cold as the sun sank. Beneath him was the solid earth. Under the soils, the inner empire of worms, slugs, arthropods, where the dark labyrinths of invertebrates met tree roots and subterranean streams, beneath the crust, beneath the lithosphere, hot currents ran. The globe's core was molten, a cauldron, a beating heart of iron and lead. He was reassured by its presence. The obscene palms waved above him, moved gently by a twilight breeze.

One day silence would fall over his mother earth. Silence would fall like night over the relics of his race, and all would be still. On the husks of rusting cars vines would creep and bloom unseen, in the temples of commerce and industry bricks would crack, ceilings would cave, dust would line the marble staircases and grass would grow through the floorboards.

Only he, Dean Decetes, would wander through the alcoves of the churches, prowl the corridors of ancient prosperity, and watch the rolling of the tides. He would sit on the rooftops and see the great flocks as they covered the sky, he would see pterodactyls blot out the sun, observe the return of the bison, the eagles, the tall-grass prairies.

He alone, misunderstood, embattled prodigal son, would prevail, with his tribe of humble survivors. The poor and the downtrodden would cleave unto him, as would the gentle animals. Even now he was bleeding into the land that had borne him. His blood was running in the soil.

—Get up guy. This is private property.

—You pondscum, man can never own the earth. Go ask the Indians.

—The Indians are dead. Now haul your indigent ass off my lot.

—In point of fact I inhabit a single-family dwelling in Culver City. You see before you a temporary victim of circumstance.

CHAPTER THE FOURTH

Houseguests run amok; a Death occurs;
Chaos begins to reign; and the Prince finds his Princess

—Come in, come in.

—Bucella, this is my wife Barbara. Barbara, my coworker Bucella.

Barbara was gangly and pigeontoed. She smiled and nodded, eyes fixing briefly on Bucella's chin and then straying toward a macrame wall hanging.

—Can I offer you a glass of wine?

—We do not drink fermented beverages or spirits, do we Barbara.

—I want a glass. Special occasion.

—No Barbara.

—Yes please. A glass of wine for me, thank you very much.

—Dinner should be ready soon. Make yourselves at home. Barbara, I understand you were in a fire last night. That must have been a terrible experience.

—Physically she is unharmed!

Barbara hovered at Bucella's elbow while she poured the wine, then drained the goblet in a gulp.

—Barbara!

7:20

Alice, in fresh underwear, wrapped the banana and fashioned a floppy bow as she listened to her messages.

—I bet you thought I would forget your name, I was so fucking shitfaced. Surprise! I smell my sheets, it's like a natural high babe. Gimme a call. —Alice? Honey? This is your mother! I got your number from the Information, I checked New York, Chicago, Dallas, then Los Angeles and you were listed. You sure are far away. I hope it's really you honey. If it's someone else I'm sorry. Ray's sick honey. He's got this colon cancer. You wanna come home Alice? I know you two didn't get along but he's real sick sweetheart. He hardly weighs a thing. He's so skinny, just skin and bones. He cain't hurt a fly. They got him on some machines at the hospital. He cain't even use a potty by hisself anymore. I'm still at the same number in Knoxville. You think about it Alice. God bless you honey. I hope you done okay for yourself.

—I knew I should have been unlisted, said Alice out loud. She put down the banana and strode to the kitchen cabinet, from which she extracted a bottle.

7:39

—My sister calls me Babs.

—Barbara's sister has recently recovered from hepatitis, said Phillip.

—Hepatitis A, said Babs. —Fishbowl with a treasure chest! I like it. We can't have a pet. They're too dirty he says.

—I do not object to fish of course, put in Phil Kreuz quickly.

—I am not fond of the fish, said Bucella. —My brother gave it to me on my birthday, for what reason I am not in a position to know.

—Yummy. More please.

—I was under the impression Barbara that you were attempting to watch your weight.

Phillip had eaten his small piece of lasagna and carefully placed his fork and knife beside each other, upside down on the edge of the plate.

—Can I get some more wine?

—Barbara, I am putting my foot down. Bucella I must ask you not to pour her any more wine.

He clasped his hands on the edge of the table. Oh my it was quite Awkward. Babs held out her goblet, fingers clenched around the stem. It wavered in the air over the casserole.

—Put that down Barbara, you are embarrassing our hostess.

—I'll get it myself.

—She is not accustomed to alcohol. Barbara you are intoxicated!

—I like beer. I drank eight beers at the party last night.

—Eight—!

Babs rose and went to the sideboard, where she poured more cabernet into her glass. Bucella kept her eyes on her plate and lanced a cherry tomato with her salad fork. Domestic Strife was drowning out Hildegarde.

—Barbara please behave. We are in Bucella's home.

—Phillip, I don't mind—

—No Bucella. This display is inappropriate. Barbara come sit down, and leave your glass where it is.

—Then let me keep Bronco Bill.

—Barbara this is neither the time nor the place.

—Let me keep Bronco Bill.

—Please Barbara. Your attitude is deeply distressing. Perhaps Bucella would like to hear about your activities with the Science and Health Inspirational Teachings Personal Initiative Group.

—No she wouldn't.

—I would be very interested, said Bucella. —Phillip, would you care for more salad?

—No thank you. Barbara this is your fourth glass, I have counted. Sit down.

—Look! said Babs, and giggled, pointing at the fishbowl. The goldfish was swimming along with a long thread of excrement trailing behind.

—That is distasteful Barbara. Nature is unappealing at the dinner table.

—Fish with a shit. It's a shitfish!

—Language Barbara! Language!

—Fishy shit and shitty fish, fishy shit and shitty fish, sang Babs, and began to hop on one leg, spilling wine on the carpet.

Phillip's hands were shaking on the table edge. He rose abruptly, laying his napkin down beside his plate.

—Barbara we will have to depart. I apologize Bucella. It is most likely an allergic reaction. I cannot tell you how irregular this is. Barbara believes in the life of the mind. She knows that Christ lives in the spirit. She has never behaved this way before. The trauma no doubt.

—Mind of Christ and shitty fish, mind of Christ and shitty fish, continued Babs singsong, and then stopped hopping long enough to empty her goblet.

—Come Barbara. We are leaving.

He took her by the arm, but she wriggled away and ran into the living room. Bucella, still seated at the head of the table, watched Phillip cross the floor and make a grab for his wife. She dodged behind the couch. He stood facing her with a frown.

—Barbara, come here, he said, lips in a tight line, gritting his teeth.

Bucella watched with bated breath as Babs came around the corner of the couch and approached him, hesitant.

—Good Barbara. Now get your purse. We are leaving.

But Babs leaned forward and Vomited.

Lordy Lord!

—It's on my shoes! cried Phillip.

He stepped backward as Babs deposited additional lasagna on the floor. Bucella ran to the kitchen to find a rag. When she got back Phillip was retreating into the bathroom and Babs was staring down at her Contribution.

—Step back please, said Bucella. The carpet had been steam-cleaned not three weeks ago.

—Shoebarf, observed Babs. —Shoebarf and rugbarf. Barf like a dog!

—Please move away from that so I can clean it up, said Bucella. —Paper towels are in the kitchen.

—Let's get the shitfish, said Babs. —That shitty fish!

—Please, step back, said Bucella, and knelt down to apply herself to the task at hand. She felt queasy herself. It was quite Horrifying. Steam-cleaned! It cost two hundred dollars. She was scrubbing when Phillip reentered the room, his slacks wet.

—Put that down! Put it down Barbara, or I will punish you severely!

—I got the shitfish and I'm going to eat it, said Babs. Bucella craned her neck to behold Babs lowering the twitching goldfish into her mouth.

—Do not swallow that fish! said Phillip, and bounded up to his wife.

Her mouth was pursed closed, the cheeks bulging. He put one hand on her jaw and tried to pry her lips open with the other. She swallowed.

—Hee hee hee! Tickly fish!

—Barbara, we are leaving this minute. Get your purse right now and follow me out the door. Please forgive her Bucella. She has lost her way.

—Yes, I—

—I'm staying! cried Babs, and fled toward the den.

Phillip pursued her while Bucella disposed of the rag in the kitchen and washed her hands. When she rejoined them Babs had scuttled under Dean's filthy sofa. One foot protruded from beneath it, promptly retracted when Phillip grabbed at it.

—Barbara, you may retain the Bronco Bill. Now will you come out?

After a minute of silence Babs inched out and righted herself. But Bucella had been unprepared. Used Prophylactics were hanging off her like tree ornaments.

—Oh Lord, they must be my brother's, said Bucella hastily, and commenced to gather them frantically off Babs's arms, back and legs. They were Filthy! But they had to come off. Phillip would think she lived in Sin. He stood staring with his arms crossed on his chest as she brushed cocoons of dirt and sediment off Babs's shoulders.

—Rubbers, stated Babs.

—That is sufficient Barbara. You will be silent.

—Spermatozoa, said Babs. —Sperm sperm sperm.

One stubborn tube was attached to the heel of her shoe. Leaning down Bucella whisked it into the palm of her hand. Where had they come from? During the day, while she was gainfully employed, he must be entertaining Loose Women. The couch was permanently Soiled.

—Sin! giggled Babs. —Sperm! A firm sperm. Sperm is firm.

—Shut your mouth!

—Firmy spermy firmy sperm.

—That's the doorbell. Why don't you get her tidied up in the bathroom? I think my brother has some pants you can wear.

It was Jerry Frenter from next door, with his tie loosened and jacket slung over one shoulder.

—There's a message on my answering machine from the LAPD. Do you know what happened to my wife?

—First she painted this on my door.

Bucella stepped onto the porch and unhooked the Thanksgiving wreath.

—Child Molester?

—Then she got into my car while I was looking at it and she almost ran over me when I tried to stop her. She drove off. I had to break my own back window to get into the house. My keys were in the car.

—Jesus! She's been in counseling. Can I come in?

—I have guests.

—We were just leaving, said Phillip, and pushed Babs out the front door ahead of him. —Bucella, you have my heartfelt apologies. It was the trauma of the fire. Barbara, get in the car.

They watched as Babs stumbled down the footpath, then made a sudden detour toward the backyard in a sprint.

—Barbara!

—Excuse me, said Jerry Frenter. —I'll come back later.

Phillip was down the steps, chasing a disappearing tail. As Jerry walked back to his house Bucella exhaled. She had to wash her hands. They bore the Stains of Dean's Vile Deeds. She was his keeper, a long-suffering Abel to his Cain, Abel who endured the seasons, the cold frosts and painful grievances without complaint, while Cain slaughtered cute little calves.

Standing over the bathroom sink, looking at the hand towels she had acquired at a church sale, embroidered His and Hers in pale-blue script, she heard a noise. Abrupt metallic crunch.

She took two Advil, dried her hands on Hers, stood with closed eyes preparing herself for further Tribulation, and walked out to the front porch again. At the curb, Dean's Pinto was piggybacked on Phillip's gray Hyundai. The back of the Hyundai was crumpled like an accordion. Dean himself lay face-down on the grass of her lawn.

—Get up this minute, she told him in stentorian tones. —I have guests. She glanced toward the side of the house, but they were nowhere to be seen. Thank the Lord.

He lay silent, unmoving. She heaved a burdened sigh and walked over, nudging his arm with her foot. He groaned.

—Dean, you will get up immediately or I will drag you myself. Your presence is unwelcome. I told you I was having guests. They will return any minute.

She leaned down and rolled him over. His face was purple, yellow and swollen. He blinked at her, then raised a blood-encrusted hand and dreamily picked his nose.

—Dean I am warning you now, if you do not get up I will drag you.

She wished to conceal him from the Kreuzes. But he was very heavy. Her brother was a dead weight. He had stopped picking his nose and seemed to be unconscious again. She squatted beside him on the grass, grabbed him under the armpits and heaved. The grass, wet with dew, was helpful.

At the porch steps, his head met concrete once or twice, but finally she had him inside. His skull was hard as a rock. As a child, he had butted it repeatedly against a table edge one day with no adverse effects. The living room couch was the only safe Haven. She tugged him behind it and tried to roll him underneath, but his bony hip struck the frame. He would have to be pushed by increments. She heard footsteps on the porch. She had his head under, his Buttocks. Then his feet, and she rose calm and collected as Phillip burst in, breathing hard.

—Did you see it? Did you see, my God! My car has been destroyed!

—My stars! How?

—I mean it's totaled!

—Where is your wife?

—I must notify the police. The driver is nowhere to be found. I will be forced to litigate! It's hit and run. You didn't see anything?

—Oh no.

—I will call the police, and then a towing service. Where is your telephone?

If Dean woke up while Phillip was in the house, all was Lost.

—It's out of order. Why don't you call from next door?

8:24

—Sure, help yourself, said Jerry Frenter, stepping back to usher them in. —Phone's in the hall. I was having a glass of sherry. Join me, Mr.—?

—I do not drink spirits. Where is it located?

—Through the kitchen, there on the right.

Phillip strode past them, stroking his mustache.

—I will have a glass, thank you. It has been an exhausting evening.

—Bar's in the basement, follow me. Installed it myself last spring. What's the deal with this guy, his pants are dripping on the floor.

—His wife was sick. Now his car has been rear-ended.

Phillip dialed. There was no answer at 911. Something was wrong, truly wrong. He hung up and dialed again. The voices of Bucella and her neighbor were distracting.

—Some fucking night. Watch your head, the ceiling's low. We can sit on the patio. My wife's gone, my daughter's gone. I have nothing to do. Dry or sweet?

—Sweet. Thank you.

An operator picked up. He could barely hear her.

—A car rear-ended me!

—Is someone injured, sir?

—No, but—

—I'll tell you honestly, she has some problems. She's seeing a counselor, but it doesn't seem to help. Of course I'll pay for the damage to your house. I'm really sorry. I'll pay for a rental car till we get this cleared up. Spare no expense. Hire yourself a Lincoln.

—Thank you, but I prefer compact cars.

—And she's codependent.

Phil saw them go through sliding doors; Bucella sat down on a lawn chair and crossed her legs.

—Just call your local police station, okay sir? They'll send an officer to make a report.

Scratchy, grainy, bad-tasting: it was Decetes's tongue that first brought the exterior back into his life. The tongue was touching burlap, above him. It was difficult to breathe. He moved a leg and pain shot through the knee. Someone had packaged him; he was being shipped in a crate, like livestock. But the smells were strangely familiar. Yes: he was in Bucella's living room, between the sofa and the floor.

There were sores, aches, but he dismissed them. The parts of time ran together, fluid. He had arrived here, but by what means? A transmigration of souls? The tragedy of all tragedies, to be someone else. He refused to believe it. But it was dark and close where he lay, like a coffin; the carpet smelled worse than usual. God's teeth! It stank of acrid bile!

He knew the odor well.

He moved sideways, into the air and light. He raised his head. He would stand. Yes: he would walk erect. He gathered his strength and made the effort, but fell back. Black holes appeared on the periphery of his vision. They spread and metamorphosed. The Little Drummer Boy was playing in his head, marching, stamping, beating on his tinny vessel with loud sticks. Decetes ordered the scamp to shut up, but he would not. Decetes made dire threats to the Drummer Boy. —I will Rum-pum-pum-pum you, he warned. The Boy refused to desist. Decetes would pummel him with a club. That would teach him. The little shit. Decetes was the Bandmaster. —I will Rum-pum-pum-pum you, he repeated.

This time the Drummer paid attention and his awful beat abated. Decetes stood, triumphant.

But he was still hallucinating. Before him squatted an awkward, dark-haired woman, naked from the waist down. Mongoloid? Possibly. She wore thick glasses and her over-large eyes were wide open, staring at him. He recalled now: it was a dream from last night. The naked woman had danced on a sidewalk. He was having recurring visions. It was a sign of glory. But what was its significance?

—What do you mean? he asked the apparition.

He was dizzy. He steadied himself on the sofa arm.

—I ate the fish, she said blankly. —The fish is inside me.

Her white thighs were dimpled and trembling. The large brown eyes gazed upon him steadfastly, unblinking. And she was speaking of fish: fish, the symbol of Christ. She was the earth mother and he was the man to lead the meek.

—Thank you, he said. —I always knew I was chosen.

No matter that he in particular was an unbeliever. This would be the crusade of the flesh, not its renunciation. Jesus himself had been Jewish.

9:00

—That's disgusting! squealed the bride-to-be. She held the vibrator aloft like a scepter. —I can't believe you bought this!

—I have the receipt, said Alice. —You can return it if you like. They put me up to it.

—Are you kidding? She's going to need it where she's going! screeched a celebrant, as Alice winced into her margarita. They were a flock of small-brained sparrows, chirping. A Chippendale clicked onto the stage in cowboy boots, black mask and spangled cloak.

—Yeah all right! cheered a bridesmaid. —Give it to us Lone Ranger!

—We need another couple of pitchers, said the bride-to-be.

—I'll get them, said Alice.

Dousing her face in cold water at the restroom sink, she remembered finding a pale rock in the riverbed, a pale flat rock, and she had dipped her hand in, raked her fingers through the wet pebbles and pulled it out. It was a sand dollar, but they were hundreds of miles from the sea.

The miracle had never been repeated.

9:22

—Bucella! Wherefore art thou goddammit?

—Oh Lord, that's my brother. He is inebriated.

Jerry Frenter was not yet acquainted with Dean.

—Bucella!

Dean's bloated face, the color of a rotting plum, materialized from the darkness of the copse.

—Dean I am having a quiet drink with Mr. Frenter here while my coworker calls triple A. You should not be here when Mr. Kreuz joins us. Why don't you go to bed and stay there.

—Jesus man, what happened to you?

—I was set upon by Philistines. But that is not important now. Bucella, I had a vision.

—What else is new Dean. Go to bed.

—Bucella it was the earth mother.

—I'm surprised Dean, it is usually a prostitute.

—Bucella I'm serious. She told me I'm chosen to lead. I've known it for some time, but it has been confirmed.

—I'll have what he's having. Excuse me, I'm getting a refill. Would you care for another glass Bucella?

—No thank you.

He closed the sliding door behind him.

—Bucella it was the earth mother. In your living room.

—There are no earth mothers in my living room.

—There was an earth mother Bucella, the same one I saw last night before the house burned down.

—Dean the house did not burn down. It is standing behind you, unburned. Now go to bed. I do not want my coworker to see you Dean. You crashed into his car. He may find out, but not from me. If I were you Dean I would hide.

—It was a big mother Bucella. Big and naked. But its mouth was the oracle, the oracle of Delphi. It told me Bucella. I am the Lamb. I am the Lion. I'm the fish.

—It was probably one of those fallen women from the videotapes, and you were dreaming about her. Now get out of here.

—You are graced Bucella. You are graced with my godhead.

—Do not be profane Dean. I never heard of godheads that left condoms under the sofa. Now leave before you end up facing litigation. I thought that thing was in an impound lot.

—I kidnapped it Bucella, I had my wits about me and my wits are keen. I am going Bucella, but remember what I have said. They will bow before me in deserts, they will weep when I touch them.

—You got that right Dean. Go!

—Bucella?

—That's him! The guy whose car you wrecked! Get out!

—Bucella, the police and California Automobile Association are on their way.

—Good Phillip. Have a seat.

—Bless you my son, you are absolved. I bid you both adieu. Vaya con Dios. Yo soy Dios. Yo soy Jesus. Be calm my good man, the flesh is willing but the spirit is weak.

—Who was that?

—A homeless person. He sometimes sleeps in the ravine.

—You must exercise caution with these individuals. They are frequently schizophrenic. Some of them carry weapons.

—That one is harmless.

Jerry Frenter stepped through the sliding door to join them, crystal decanter and glass in hand.

—Oh, he left?

—Yes he's gone. Let's not talk about him.

10:06

Wedged between Alice and a plaster gladiator painted gold was a middle-aged woman in a ratty, peach-velour caftan. Her chin was partly submerged in a daiquiri. Alice leaned forward on the bar and gently touched her shoulder. She jerked up, spilling pink slush.

—Sorry, said Alice, and plied a cocktail napkin to the spill. —Are you okay?

10:31

—Yes Officer. Hit and run.

—The car is registered to you sir?

—My wife. For insurance reasons.

—We'll need a statement from her.

—Yes Officer. Unfortunately she is indisposed. Let me show you the damage.

The policeman followed Phillip down to the curb. Jerry Frenter stood beside Bucella on the porch, his sherry glass in hand, sipping as he watched the proceedings.

—I've seen that car here before, he said slowly. —That car belongs to your brother.

—He drives it, but its ownership is uncertain, said Bucella. —I cannot be involved. It has been a long day.

—Who is that? Jesus!

—That is my coworker's wife.

—But she's—

—Barbara?

—She's not wearing—

—Barbara!

—I found the Smurf!

Barbara was gallumphing down the driveway from the backyard wearing only her blouse and carrying a gnome garden statuette. The gnome was wearing a blue cap. Phillip trotted awkwardly behind her, trying to herd her toward the house with sweeping arm gestures.

—The Smurf is with me!

—Barbara, get inside! Now! Please do not arrest her Officer. It is a chemical imbalance. Barbara, inside!

She held the painted gnome in a tight hug as she trundled up the front steps. Bucella and Jerry Frenter stepped back to let her pass. Jerry's mouth was hanging open.

—Jesus.

—She is mentally challenged, whispered Bucella.

The spectacle was unpleasant. What could possibly explain the marriage? Phillip had set himself the task of taming a heathen. He was a missionary, a Healer. Yes. He had crosses to bear. She had her own. She knew. They were both Oxen at the plow, with heavy shoulders and sad eyes.

—Excuse me, she told Jerry. —I will offer them my assistance.

But Lordy Lord! Dean might be in there. Lying in wait for them.

10:30

—May I buy you a drink? asked the old skinny guy.

—Maybe just a soda, said Ginny. —Um, Coke I guess.

—Mike! Coke here. Will you tell me your name?

—Ginny, she said. —What's yours?

—Alan. My nickname's sort of Alan H.

—Are you married Alan H.?

—No, said the old guy. —I was once, but not now.

—Got a girlfriend?

—No. No I don't.

—Then can I crash at your place tonight? she asked, twisting a strand of hair over her eye.

The old guy looked like he won the lottery.

10:44

—Let's get out of here, said Alice.

—But I haven't met the male strippers, said Riva.

—Come on. We'll go somewhere else. I'll lend you a change of clothes.

—Change, murmured Riva.

10:45

—This is where I live, said Alan H.

—I like it, said Ginny.

It was definitely swank, in some kind of black-and-white, leather way. She picked a good one, considering. The guy was kind of sad though, old and sad. —Can I get another soda? Actually my favorite is Dr. Pepper. Do you have Dr. Pepper?

Decetes stepped onto the patio of the businessman with the slut daughter. The glass sliding door was open. He went in. A bar, saints be praised. An open liquor cabinet in the businessman's basement.

He poured himself a whiskey and sat down in a leather recliner, swinging his feet up onto the padded footrest. Providence shone on his head like the sun. She opened her arms and clasped him to her breasts, she spread her legs and let him rest his head in the sweet salty cradle of jungle and sea. The moors were his, the waters, the steeples, the dunes. His home was every home. He swished a gulp in his mouth, savored it and swallowed. This was better whiskey than he usually drank. He would do well to cultivate the man's acquaintance.

—The earth mother visits me, he told the Chivas Regal solemnly. —She offers me an empire of light.

Footsteps. Decetes decided to brazen it out.

—Taking you up on that drink you offered me, he said, when the businessman entered the room.

—So you totaled some guy's car, said the businessman.

—The brakes went out, said Decetes.

—Uh huh, said the businessman. —Ready for another?

—Delighted.

The businessman took the bottle by the neck and filled Decetes's crystal tumbler.

—Notice you favor blended whiskeys, said Decetes, making genial small talk. —Single-malt man, myself. But to each his own. Bottoms up.

Heaving a sigh, the businessman sat down on the couch to down half his drink and then slap one knee with a square hand. Decetes noticed he was wearing a bulbous gold Rolex.

—Nice watch you got there.

—Thanks. Used to be my old man's.

—My old man had a crappy Seiko, said Decetes.

—Ha ha, said the businessman, and sipped.

—I saw your wife outside this morning, said Decetes.

—Jesus I hate it when she goes out in that fucking robe, said the businessman, and reached for the bottle again. —Got her a new one but she refuses to wear it.

—Apricot is not the best color for her, said Decetes, sipping. —She's a winter.

—My wife thinks you're a Peeping Tom. Are you a Peeping Tom?

—My God, said Decetes, and shook his head sadly. —How the mighty have fallen. I used to be an account manager over at Shearson Lehman, before it was Smith Barney. Lost a shitload in the crash of '87 and they fired me. The ball just won't roll for me anymore, and here the neighbors think I'm a Peeping Tom. Kicking a man when he's down.

—I never thought you were, said the businessman, sitting forward. —I swear. My wife's neurotic, that's all.

—It's just, said Decetes, —you have this momentum. And then someone pulls the rug out, and you never get your balance again. I used to have clients like Leona goddamn Helmsley.

—Are you kidding?

—I swear. She parceled out her assets to dozens of places. I had a slice of the pie.

—Why didn't you go to another brokerage house?

—They blackballed me, said Decetes sadly.

—Jesus. I'm in merchandising, myself.

—I took risks in futures and '87 was the first time they didn't pan out, said Decetes. —Been out in the cold ever since.

—Jesus.

—You got that right, said Decetes, shaking his head again.

A liberal supply of Chivas was assured.

—You ever play golf? asked the businessman.

11:15

—Alice! You came! Like my dress?

—It's lovely. This is my new friend Riva. We just met in a bar. She's having some problems at home.

—Hello Riva. What a creative dress. I'm Lola. This is Jerome.

—Jerome, I've heard so much about you, said Alice.

—Oh dear, said Jerome. He kissed her on both cheeks and then kissed Riva's hand. Alice could tell she was blushing. Riva was a chicken in the land of vultures. Disoriented, aimless. In need of strength, but there was only company to offer.

—We have to get backstage, said Ernest as Lola. —The show's about to start. See you ladies later.

—Can I have a drink with umbrellas in it?

—Barkeep? Give her a Shirley Temple.

—I love the little umbrellas. Maybe I'll collect them.

—Everyone should have a hobby, said Alice.

—Jerry says I'm codependent.

11:21

—You want me to what? asked Ginny.

She was looking down at him with her knees on both sides of his hips. It was dark so she could hardly see his face. Creepy. Just the sheet and the white rope.

—Pull it tighter, breathed Alan H. —More. Don't be shy. Pull it tighter. As tight as you can.

—As tight as I can? asked Ginny. —What if it hurts?

—I want it to.

The knot was against his Adam's apple. They weren't even moving, he was just there like part of her.

—I don't know, she said. —I've never done weird stuff before.

—Please, whispered Alan H. —I couldn't ask for more.

—Is that tight enough? she said.

—Tighter, said Alan H. —Tighter.

—But are you sure it won't hurt, she said.

—I want it to hurt, whispered Alan H. —If thine eye offend thee, pluck it out.

—What?

—I am the eye.

—I don't get it!

She was scared. He must be crazy. She let the cord loosen.

—Don't! I only want this.

—You can't breathe! Can you?

—Don't be afraid, he rasped. —You're only a baby. In the woods.

—Please can I stop, she said. She was starting to cry like a wimp. He had his hands on her hips and held her there, but pretty softly. —I want to stop okay.

—Please don't. I've been waiting for this all my life.

He was moving a little now like a boat on the water, rocking.

—Please, she said.

—Forgive me, I'm sorry, he said. —But I need a baby. It has to be a baby.

He could hardly talk, he was rasping and out of breath. *Square root 75, 8.66. Square root 114, 10.677.*

—Please! That's enough right? Okay?

—I just want to be gone, he whispered, —just a little bit gone, and he took his hands off her hips and put them over her own on the ends of the rope, trembling. He pulled hard. Suddenly.

11:31

Standing on the curb, Bucella watched them hitch up the Hyundai and crank it onto the truck. The Kreuzes seated themselves stiffly in the cab, shoulder to shoulder. Babs snaked one arm out the passenger window and waved gaily as the tow truck pulled away. Bucella retreated to her kitchen and washed dishes. The gnome garden statuette was lying on its side on the linoleum under the breakfast table. A swear-word heralded her brother's presence.

—Dean, she told him, when he appeared tottering in the doorframe beneath her ceramic Love Is . . . plate, —you are no longer welcome here.

—Bucella you know not whereof you speak, said Dean. —It is I who will bring greatness to our family name. You should cozen up to me while you still can.

—I mean it, you're evicted, said Bucella. —Tomorrow.

—Let us sleep on it, Bucella, said Dean, and fell on his face where he stood.

CHAPTER THE FIFTH

The Innocent becomes confused; a Comedy of Errors ensues;
and the Prince among men is rudely dethroned

THURSDAY MORNING
7:42

Ginny poured cereal into a bowl and added milk. The fridge had an icemaker in the door. She pressed a button and watched ice cubes skitter across the floor, then picked up her bowl and stepped around them carefully. Her hands were shaking weirdly. There was a big-screen TV in the living room. Jonah T.'s dad had a big-screen TV till Jonah T. broke it with a barbell.

She sat down on the couch and spooned up cereal, looking at the gray square. She didn't turn it on. Her reflection was in the gray square but it was like she was a whole other person. A grownup but also a ghost. No colors only gray. Her face was lines with a hollow middle. She watched the hollow lines eat the cereal. Then it was gone. She drank the milk and looked at the empty bowl. Then she had to go back to the bedroom.

Mr. Alan was still on the bed, on his back, with his arms out. His eyes were closed and his face was puffy, and kind of blue around the lips like in *Law and Order*. But that was all fake too. She sat down on the floor to wait for him to wake up. She was tired from waiting all night and no sleeping but it was like she took NoDoz except she hadn't taken NoDoz. She held the bowl in her lap and watched her hands shake. She couldn't help it. Some unseen force was moving them like on *Sightings*.

8:14

—I would like to return some merchandise, said Phillip, with more common courtesy than the fleshmongers deserved.

The manufacturers' toll-free telephone number was printed upon the shipping label; he was striking while the iron was hot. Though it was 8:14 a.m., Barbara was lounging in debauched slumber. Her excesses were wanton. She lay on her back with her legs thrown out, two white pods resembling sausages at the meat counter, and snored noisily. That was where he had first caught sight of her: in the section marked FROZEN FOODS. She had round eyes and small feet pointed in at each other, and was holding a grocery list printed in capital letters. Like the shepherd with a lost lamb he had gathered her in.

During the night, after they returned and he bathed himself at some length using no fewer than three bars of antibacterial soap, he had taken stock of the situation. She was a wolf in sheep's clothing. At first he had taken her naivete for a pleasant attribute, a warm void awaiting the infusion of spirit. But it was abundantly clear now that she would never be a testimonial. She was the brutish force of animal mass, and nothing more.

Thank the Lord that thus far, in the eighteen months of their conjugal alliance, he had prudently withheld consummation. While the flesh was merely a rotten vessel, there were vessels and then there were vessels.

—Bronco Bill is the name of the item. It must be picked up here today, and taken away.

—What are you doing? she screeched, blundering out of the bedroom with her arms outstretched.

—I will place a key under the doormat. Please be prompt.

8:53

Alice left the housewife asleep on her couch, where she'd collapsed in the small hours, flopping and mumbling in a haze of tropical mixed drinks, clutching paper parasols. On her way past the trash she dumped the soiled velour robe. It had the slack, heavy feel of wet fur, the shucked skin of a doe fallen dead in the rain.

The drive-thru menuboard read HASH BROWNS, CHEESE DANISH, speckled with birdshit.

—May I take your order, rasped an underpaid voice from the speakerbox.

—Black coffee that's all thanks and I know the total, said Alice, and released the handbrake to coast downhill to the window.

—Cream with that?

—No thanks just black, said Alice, and forked over the coin of the realm. It happened every single day. She always enunciated clearly. Black coffee, she said. But ears were growing obsolete from disuse. They would atrophy soon and fall off. The man of the future would be featureless save for his mouth.

9:11

The surface of a liquid was perfectly level unless something moved it. Matter into energy wasn't always life, but life was always matter into energy. Or something. Anyway life was movement. At least in Math PSAT Preparation.

She got up and set the bowl on his bare stomach, and then walked back to the kitchen. She took the milk carton out of the fridge and carried it to the bed. Then she poured milk into the bowl, until it overflowed and ran down the sides of his stomach, wetting the sheets. Then she stopped and waited, staring at the milk in the bowl. Not a ripple.

9:43

—Goddammit where is everybody? asked Alice of the empty office, and dumped the cold contents of her drive-thru cup into a ficus pot.

She walked into Ernie's room to get a coffee filter, saw a memo to Phil on the desk with a manila envelope beside it, and picked them up. Ernie had worn his spangled pumps into the ground. His exuberant tango had won him a standing ovation and a broken heel. He would come in late. She dropped the papers on Phil's chair as she passed it.

10:02

—This is an egregious error, said Decetes. —Do you know who I am?

—Yeah, do you? said the security guard, and peeled Saran Wrap off a greasy egg-filled croissant. —Alan H. let you go. You're fired, bro. No admittance.

In the lobby downstairs Decetes stood staring at the gold and black flecks in the tile. It was high-rent flypaper dotted with corpses. Pay some candyass decorator enough cash to feed a thousand bloat-bellied brats in Namibia, he gave you flies in the floor for your trouble and lounged beside his heated pool comparing fabric swatches till the cows came home.

When Decetes finally lifted his gaze, in a trance, there was a dwarf staring at him. A flabby lower lip and a sprouting growth upside the nose, wrinkled and lobed like a brain. The dwarf wore his stringy brown hair in a pigtail.

—Decetes! Decetes it's me! Remember me? Ken!

A toy soldier was better than none.

—Ken! Let me shake your hand. You are free.

—Free Decetes and ready to meet the naked ladies like you promised me.

—First Ken, we have errands to run. Then the naked ladies. You must fill the tank of my car. It has run out of gas. The Pinto beside the NO PARKING sign Ken, the wild horse on the plain.

—Get gas?

—On the corner there is a Texaco. I can see the red and white star Ken, the red star of morning. She beckons to you. Bring back a jug of gas Ken, and please make it snappy. We have work before us.

—But—

—Ken a great book is opening its pages to you. Ken that book is named history. Now run along.

The telephone rang on the bedside table. Ginny was dressing from the walk-in closet. She felt dreamy. Listless, from Vocabulary P-SAT. She put on one of his shirts and let the answering machine pick up as she buttoned. —Alan, you taking a sick day or something? I gotta know. Alan I'm too busy for this shit.

She stood rooted to the spot, the big shirt hanging almost to her knees. Everything was blank. Her hands were shaking and there was milk going sour on the skin of his stomach with its curling hairs. If she closed her eyes she would fall down from dizziness, but keeping them open was terrible, the brightness and hardness of the lines. Fermat's principle. Angle of incidence equals angle of reflection. Light takes the shortest path to its object. *If angle x = 0, sine x = 0 and cosine x = 1. If x = π/6, sine x = .5 and cosine x = 1.73205/2 = .866025. If x = π/4, sine x = 1.414213/2 = .707106 and cosine x is the same.*

11:04

—Keep 'em guessing, remarked Decetes to himself as he screwed a purloined license plate onto the bracket. The Pinto had emerged unscathed from last night's encounter: it had beat the Hyundai in a fair fight. Detroit had triumphed over Tokyo. For once.

And now Ken had arrived. Decetes would lay tasks upon him like bales of hay on a forklift. Already he was visible in the distance, bearing his burden of unleaded fuel. Ken must keep a low profile; he was not charismatic per se. Not his fault, of course, and he was a stouthearted fellow. And of course, as the saying went, behind every great man there is a gutless convict.

Decetes let him fill the tank and then occupy the backseat. Ken's attention was claimed by the treasure trove of old magazines, which he pored over as Decetes drove. —At play in the fields of the whores, said Decetes.

Ken jerked his head up from the glossy pages, nodding with a glassy-eyed stare.

—As you can see I have quite a library, continued Decetes. —To which you, Ken, will have unlimited access.

—They passed it around, guys only got to see it for a—

—Forget the days of scarcity my friend. This is the lode.

—Not even time—

—Yes yes. But all is not wine and roses yet my boy.

—A one-way street?—

—The laws of common men are not our laws Ken. You should know that right off the bat. We're going to my sister's. I have personal effects there, and considerable financial resources.

—Wide load!—

—Faith my boy, faith. I'm the captain of this ship. You see we squeezed by him there, not a scratch on our chassis.

—But the side of the—

—Now. The power and the glory, Ken. Before we cement this alliance I need a promise from you. Loyalty. Ken, you must promise to be loyal. There can only be one sheriff in every town, and here that sheriff's name is Dean Decetes.

—But uh . . . promise what, Decetes?

—Oh Ken. Ken Ken Ken.

— . . . mean is it like a club?

—A club, a secret society Ken, yes. You could call it that. The next empire Ken, the thousand-year Reich, the new kingdom so to speak. Are you with me?

—Nazis?

—Ken Ken Ken. There are no Nazis here Ken. Do you see a Nazi Ken?

—Watch the lady!

—Reich, it's a manner of speaking. Just means government Ken. I am no fan of monsters, tyrants, or morons Ken. No sir, they're not for me. You hungry m'boy? Find us an eatery. Ribs, chicken, steakhouse, like that. Take us to lunch Ken.

—Take?—

—Pay you back later Ken, when we get to my sister's.

—Sure okay. I guess.

They pulled into a Sizzler. Other patrons looked askance at Ken. No matter: again, he was stouthearted, if stunted in growth. Decetes ordered a steak.

—A little history Ken. What were you in for again?

—Armed robbery, assault with a deadly—

—You know strength then don't you Ken.

—It was wrong but see the judge said I was competent to stand trial. See cause if I hadna been competent—

—No Ken, make no excuses.

—Because see my public defender said I wasn't competent. He was a stupid defender. Hate that defender!

—Here we go, you had a steak platter and the burger was for you sir?

—Give me that, m'boy. The burger is for him.

—Don't call me boy.

—Oh ho! A gratuity will not be forthcoming. I am a man, you are a boy. The epithet was not racial. Ken, we have business before us.

—But uh—my French fries?

—Get 'em yourself you midget freak.

—Forget the fries Ken. We will have him fired on our way out.

— . . . just the fries—

—What's your IQ Ken? Can you tell me that?

—20/20 . . . ?

—Forget it Ken. Damn his eyes I asked for medium rare.

—Don't wanna make trouble—

—Trouble? We're building a new country Ken, founding a dynasty of better men.

— . . . ketchup?

—Better watch your back you bigot-ass shit, hissed the waiter as he swooped by with a tray of chicken tenders.

Ken mixed ketchup and mustard into an orange soup on his plate.

—Are you with me so far Ken?

—Put too much mustard. Tangy. Need more ketchup.

—What I'm suggesting, Ken? Religion and politics should be one and the same. Won't work with your Judeo-Christian shit, your pantheistic animal-worship hippie crap, your Jihad-loving Arabs Ken. Won't work with your half-assed so-called fledgling democracies Ken, your military regimes, your failed socialist oligopoly assfucks, your idiots like Mao killing the sparrows or melting down pots, your capitalist giants leeching the poor and denuding the land Ken. Oh no. That much is clear Ken. Only one thing everyone's got in common Ken, it's why we're here and it's the name of the game. Do you know what that is Ken?

—Food?

—No Ken no, not everyone has food. The sex drive Ken. Sex.

—Yeah, said Ken, a piece of hamburger lodged in the gap between his front teeth. —Yeah. Sex.

11:39

Ginny found a measuring tape in a desk drawer. Dimensions, light and heat. Trigonometry. Assumptions: level curves and linearity. Behind every single thing was its own math. The math of the most basic thing went on forever.

It wasn't that gross. Yeah he was old, but he was thin and he wore a leather jacket like a music guy. Plus he was nice until the weirdass sex. He said, *Take whatever you want of mine. Everything here is for you if you want it,* he said.

And he pulled it. He pulled the rope.

And then there was the sound of a crack.

Measuring from the corner of the bed to the ceiling she had to stand on the bed, which made it bounce and Mr. Alan move. He was kind of still smiling. Maybe he was in a trance state like on *X-Files.*

She tried to look at him. By now he should have been gone like digits, faded into small dots. It was mean of him to stay there. She clenched her teeth and wanted to hit him, but then her arms felt loose and couldn't even hit paper.

The bowl was still on his stomach and she couldn't stand to move it. There was something wrong with it. The milk was the same milk she drank at home when she ate her Life in the morning. But it was strange milk.

11:57

Brushing past carrels and bulletin boards, Alice caught Garfield the cat in the periphery of her sight. And then there were the Mayan ruins. Coffee splashed out of her mug onto her fingers. Bucella had plucked the postcard from Alice's trashcan, where she'd dumped it as soon as she read it. A dead civilization could cast a pall on a day. Ring around the rosy, we all fall down.

She set her cup on her desk and wiped her hand on the back of a chair, leaving brown beads on the vinyl. She felt asleep. Every morning she woke up and knew there was a ritual ahead, repetitive motion. Beyond that she didn't know what there was. You had to work. Divide and conquer! But they were all born divided. Why was it so unbearable? *Alone alone alone.* The world screamed it.

She'd been cast as Princess Division in an fourth-grade play: *The Court of King Arithmetic.* She remembered feeling proud. Division was more graceful than subtraction, multiplication or addition. They were the ugly sisters to her Cinderella. She had a crown with a silver ÷ on it, and wore a pink dress donated by the Junior League.

CHAPTER THE SIXTH

Crimes are committed; ancient Egypt plays a role; me take refuge in Sins of the Flesh; vengeance is plotted; and a noble Soul meets a sad end

THURSDAY AFTERNOON
12:11

—Very good Ken. You finished? The bill? You take care of that Ken, I'll bring the car around. Make a stop at The Quiet Man after we go by my sister's.

—Quiet Man?

—A drinking establishment Ken. A bar.

—I don't drink, I—

—Never say never. Life is short Ken. They got a machine there, you move around a hook above some stuffed animals, try to pick 'em up on the hook, if you grab 'em you win 'em. You'd like that Ken. Wouldn't you.

—I don't—

—Good man Ken. I'll meet you outside.

—But I don't know if I got enough dollars here it's—

Decetes was out the door.

—You disgraced me. There will have to be changes. I will not allow filth in my home. I will not permit it. It is the life of the spirit, Barbara, that sustains and replenishes. You were drunk and disorderly. Barbara you have no morality.

—All I did was have a glass of wine and get sick, and all I want is Bronco Bill!

—Not one glass, Barbara. Many glasses.

—Okay I got a little tipsy. But I gotta keep Bronco Bill. Be the best possible me! You *promised*!

—A promise made under duress is not really a promise, Barbara.

—It is too! It is too a promise!

She was flailing with her fists. She must be contained. He had only called in sick for half of the day. He was going to be tardy. He pinned her arms against the wall.

—Stop it! It hurts!

—Shut up Barbara! Now shut up!

—I'll scream and scream! You promised!

He was perspiring. He held both her wrists with his right hand and fumbled in the drawer of the telephone table with his left until he found his roll of duct tape.

—Eeeee! Eeee ee ee—

—There Barbara. Do you see? There will be no more filth in this house.

12:39

On *Nature* some animals played dead to fool other animals into not eating them. If stupid animals could do it, so could he.

Ginny found a razor in the vanity. She picked up a can that said GILLETTE WILD RAIN SHAVING GEL and took it to the bedroom. A guy like Mr. Alan wouldn't want his head shaved. If he didn't notice that, he was definitely not faking. She squirted gel along the hairline on the forehead.

It took a while and was kind of hard and she got hair and foam all over her hands which was disgusting. He was bald like Mr. Clean.

—Okay Mr. Alan, she said, and shook him by his rubber shoulders. They had gone cool from the A/C. —I'm not gonna eat you. Wake up Mr. Alan! Wake up please wake up!

Then it was weird how she was crying. Hot rain inside her head that came out. The bald head looked like this guy with cancer on Lifetime Television for Women.

The hot rain kept going and she huddled on the floor to stay dry.

12:47

Dean was rifling through her desk. Behind him a dirty midget hovered, with long greasy hair in a ponytail, bent over, shuffling his feet. He wore a stained gray suit and filthy Adidas with untied laces. He appeared to be homeless, a Derelict. Poor midget. It was hard to be small. But still. She did not know whether it was his or Dean's body odor that filled the room, but the Stench was overpowering.

—Dean!

The midget jumped and turned. Lordy! A horrible Wart! It covered half his cheek, jutting out from the side of his nose. He had hair growing out of his ears.

—Don't bother us Bucella.

—Don't bother you Dean? This is my house, Dean! And I'm running late! That's my private desk! Get away from it.

—She is not one of us, said Dean to his newest friend.

—What are you doing in my desk, Dean.

—Reclaiming what is mine.

—Nothing is yours. What are you holding, Dean? Scrunched up in the palm of your hand? Stamps? Is that a roll of stamps, Dean? *My* roll of stamps, Dean?

She moved forward, reaching out for it.

—These stamps resemble your stamps but are in actuality mine. One stamp looks much like the next. Stamps are not one-of-a-kind, Bucella. A stamp is not the Mona—

—You never bought a stamp in your life. Hand them over and give me back my housekey.

—All right Bucella, you drive a hard bargain, here are the stamps I'll let you have them this time. I will absorb the loss Bucella. Charity is my middle name. But about the housekey, I beg your forbearance here Bucella, but I was wondering—

—No Dean. I told you, you're evicted.

—I am turning over a new leaf Bucella, I need my sister in these times of reevaluation, of rejuvenation and rebirth. I have seen the error of my ways Bucella, I am a new man, Ken here is going to help me, right Ken? I am taking initiative. What is family for, Bucella, if not for this, a little compassion in moments of crisis?

—Don't give me that speech again, Dean.

—Speech, these words are from the heart Bucella.

—Please. The key.

—Ken, go get yourself a Coke. They're in the fridge.

—I'm not . . .

—Go, Ken! A Coke will do you good.

—Okay . . .

He clasped his hands in front of him and bent his head like a contrite little boy. The stinky Midget ambled out of the room.

—Bucella, don't make me beg here. You don't want to see me cry do you Bucella?

—I don't mind.

—So cold, so cold—the ice sister, Bucella! The ice queen! We used to play the game remember, you were the ice queen and I was the king, when the old man was wasted?

—I don't want to reminisce Dean.

—The time he cut your hair off, shaved you bald Bucella you were ten, what did I do Bucella? What did I do for you then?

—You made me a crown.

—I made you a crown! So you could be the ice queen. A crown Bucella!

They stood silent, their faces turned to the light from the window.

—Did I protect you then? I did. What did I do when he locked you in the bathroom Bucella? Did I climb up on the fire escape Bucella? Did I pass you food through the window? For two weeks? Did I feed you Bucella? When he broke your finger Bucella what did I do then? When he broke your finger, was I the doctor Bucella? Did I kiss the finger Bucella? Did I kiss the finger?

—But you've changed since then.

—A man has many troubles Bucella. It takes a worried man, to sing a worried song.

—You always do this!

—I know Bucella, I'm not always the man I would like to be. You can help me be that man, Bucella.

—But the drinking. You're just like him.

—Bucella, a cruel word. You kick a man when he's down. Your support, that's all I need. Your love.

—Dean . . . .

—Is that so much to ask? You're all I have Bucella.

—All right Dean, okay. Jerry Frenter's waiting to drive me to the car rental place. You can stay for now. But behave yourself.

—Okay Bucella. Your word is my command.

Ken shuffled in with a Pepsi in hand.

—No Coke.

12:58

—Calm down, calm down, said Alice, leaning her cheek on the receiver as she lit a cigarette. She got up and opened a window to flush out the smoke before the others came in. Little Bo Peep had lost her sheep. —Here's what you do. I left you a key, so you can get in and out. Wear my clothes. There's some cash on the counter. First you call your husband. If your daughter hasn't come home, go to the police station and file a report.

—She has my car!

—Good, so they can look for the car. Give them the license plate number and a description. You call me when you get back, and we'll decide what to do next.

—My Lord! You're smoking in the office!

—I have to go, said Alice. —You have the number here. Hanging up, she stubbed out the cigarette. —Sorry Bucella. I was hoping no one would catch me. How was your dinner party?

—It did not work out. Phillip's wife vomited on my carpet. It was newly cleaned.

—How rude, said Alice.

—She had a seizure or breakdown or something. And my car was stolen.

—Mercy Bucella. We live in a lawless society.

—Good morning Alice. Bucella. The Los Angeles Police Department is an incompetent bureaucracy. They confirmed that the automobile that hit me was stolen, but when they went to impound it this morning it was gone. I will lodge a formal complaint.

—What did I tell you Bucella, said Alice. —Lawlessness. Society is crumpling like a rotten fruit.

Phillip retreated to his cubicle.

—Have you seen Ernest this morning?

—He's not in yet, said Alice. —Why?

—I had a question, said Bucella.

—He was out late last night, said Alice.

—Out?

—Out, said Alice, and smiled.

Schoolgirl crushes. Alice remembered them, barely. The warm diffuse light of nostalgia, enclosing memory like a globe. Ignorance was bliss. That was before the world flattened out, flattened into a parking lot. There were still mountains on the horizon then, with more behind them, unknown and brilliant in the shadows.

1:02

—John gimme another draft here for myself.

—Look Decetes, I didn't want to embarrass you in front of your little friend but I heard about your conduct in here the other night with Len. You may or may not know I'm part owner of this bar, did you know that Decetes?

—No in fact, no. You see that? That guy who just passed had a parakeet on his shoulder. Saint Francis of fucking Assisi.

—What I was saying, Decetes, was this: I am part owner of the bar, and as such I have come to a decision. You can finish this drink, it's on me, but after that I want you to pick up and get out of here. And take your little friend with you. You're not welcome at The Quiet Man anymore. You can't talk that way to our staff.

—I was as sober as a judge. The man was refusing to serve me!

—You have a crappy attitude.

—Customer is always right, here you are critiquing patrons' personalities, is that the way to run a business John? Didn't you take Management 101 at community college?

—This is a case in point Decetes. Now unless you're planning to forgo the free beer I suggest you shut up.

—Fine, said Decetes primly. He grabbed the handle and quaffed. —No skin off my nose, spend my pin money elsewhere won't I John.

—You do that.

From the back of the bar came a long scream of rage. A crash and another voice. John leapt over the end of the bar. Decetes followed, beer in hand. The guy who'd come in with the bird stood in the doorway to the men's room, his back against the open door. He was bucking and jumping, leaping forward into the bathroom and then back, his arms raised. —Stop! Jesus! Jack—!

—What is it? asked John, and Ken spun into view holding a sodden feathered lump. He smashed it against the wall of the stall, leaving a smear of blood on the gray metal. Feathers whirled, a blue and yellow blizzard. Decetes craned his neck. Ken was a whirling dervish, spit around his mouth.

—Rat you damn r-r-rat! he gurgled, and smashed it again on the side of the stall, while the other guy screamed.

—Drop it Ken, drop it, said Decetes.

—Call the cops, yelled John in the direction of the bar.

—Drop it Ken, come on, said Decetes. —Come *on!*

Ken's eyes darted right and left. After a moment he hunkered down and dropped the bird, whose brain matter seemed to be braceleting his right wrist.

—I'll take care of him, calm him down, said Decetes quickly, and leaned forward, collaring Ken. —Come on my boy, under his breath, —cops are coming you don't want to go back inside do you? Stick with me.

—You bastard, sobbed the bird owner, —How could you do that? What the fuck is wrong with you?

—Drinking, said Ken. He was calming down. Decetes pulled him by the arm. —Can't drink.

—Easy now Ken, come with me.

—Allergic reaction, is what, said Ken to Decetes. —I get it when I drink, I get a little crazy, but it's over fast see? Now I'm normal.

—Jack little Jack. Jack my friend, my feathered friend.

—Ken we gotta move or you'll be doing community service for the ASPCA, working on the chain gang building bird feeders Ken. Can you run Ken? Can you run?

They passed the line of barstools, stunned patrons turning to stare, Decetes's hand on Ken's head, pat pat.

—Now when I say go you break for the door, you got that Ken? whispered Decetes.

—John have the guy arrested! Jesus Christ—!

—Go!

—Stop the midget, he killed Jack the Sailor! Hareem! Stop him!

—I said go Ken! Go!

They began their sprint, but Decetes slipped on a napkin, napkins everywhere and Ken was outside. Decetes picked himself up again and had to push Hareem out of the way.

—Sorry Sahib, said Decetes, and he was through the door and in the clear.

The Quiet Man clientele did not know their lord and master; they did not recognize his strength. They failed to see the nimbus atop his head, the swords of power jangling at his hips.

1:22

Phillip retired to the restroom to reread the letter in the manila envelope. Alone in the sanctum sanctorum. His heart was palpitating. He was short of breath.

We are trapped in our earthly Bodies, these mundane Forms, we must bring them together—

The delta of Venus, blond and discreet. Alice had shown it to him yesterday. On purpose, that was obvious in retrospect. The cradle of creation, bowl to his staff. The small place hid itself like a shy animal, coy and furtive. Awaiting baptism. Together.

—and dance a holy Dance, the dance of Life itself while He looks on smiling Above us.

Above us. Earthly bodies together. Penetration. Above her. Love is God's Gift. Above her. The letter jiggling. Words blurred.

1:28

They were showing *Cleopatra Empress of the Nile.* Normally she didn't like documentaries but this one was cool. She watched with the Kleenex box on her lap for when she kept crying and hiccuping by accident.

They showed how Cleopatra captured the imagination of numerous dramatists, and a reenactment of her being bit by a snake. Anyway he pulled the rope so it wasn't her fault. She was only a catalytic agent. Chemistry P-SAT. She caused a reaction but it wasn't her fault only her properties. He pulled the rope till when he was choking and then he went soft.

Cleopatra wore a lot of makeup. She didn't do her eyeliner too good.

1:34

—Yeah Phil, what can I do for you, said Alice. Her phone was ringing. She swung her legs down from the desk and swiveled her back to him. —Wait a sec. Lemme get this, it's an outside line. Hello?

—I was just going out your door when this lady called, I gave her your work number okay? Jerry hasn't seen Ginny and she's not at school so I'm going to talk to the police like you said.

—Fine Riva, good luck, said Alice. —Talk to you later. Dammit Phil, the other line is going. Was it something quick?

—Oh, said Phil, shifting from one foot to the other. —Would you like to have a late lunch?

—Sorry, let me just get this, okay? Hello?

—Is that Alice? Honey?

—Jesus. Mother?

—Alice, honey. Twelve years! Alice . . . .

Alice fumbled in her bag for the cigarette pack.

—Sorry Phil, I have to do this. Would you open a window?

—I don't—

—I mean it Phil! Mother, God. Do you think maybe, could we talk when I get home? Can I call you back or something?

—Sure but honey I just wanted to let you know, Ray passed away this morning.

Alice burned her thumb on the match.

—You know, I just wanted you to know honey.

—Alice, these premises are nonsmoking.

—Shut up Phil, my father just died.

—My Lord! I-I—

—Alice I wanted to tell you the funeral is in two days honey. Alice sweetheart could you come home for the service?

—Phil can I have a little privacy please? Sorry mother we have these shitty little cubicles. Can we not talk about this right now? I'd rather call you when I get home.

—You promise Alice? You promise you'll call?

—I'll call.

—Because Alice . . . honey I'm all alone . . . .

—Don't cry mother, please don't cry.

—I jist, I'm all alone . . . .

—Please don't cry, all right? I'm sorry you're alone, I really am. I don't want you to cry. Are you going to stop crying? You don't need to cry. I mean it's okay to cry. I'm—I mean I'm listening.

—If you would just come for the service . . . .

—I don't want you to be alone, but you know how it was with him and me. You know how it was.

—Please Alice . . . .

It was easy to extend every courtesy to the dead. They were always polite.

—Don't cry. I want to talk to you about this later. Don't be alone, okay? How about your friends from church? Is Marietta with you?

—Marietta passed, honey. She got a tumor in her eyeball.

2:36

Decetes and Ken were seated in the Pinto in a Vons parking lot, watching a bag lady with rats'-nest hair scour a dumpster for goodies. Decetes wielded a forty-ounce.

—Next stop Ken, a trade emporium I know. Exchange a few trinkets Ken, get some cash to produce our new movie.

His grandfather had been a coin collector. He had spent his own legacy when he was fourteen, but fortunately Bucella had kept hers.

—Let's go Ken, look at the magazines more later.

He got out, slamming the Pinto's front door, and opened the back for Ken.

—Devil where'd you put the babies? Devilman! Suckass!

The bag lady was closing on them fast, waving an egg carton.

—My dear lady please be calm, said Decetes, raising his hands, palms up. —You are clearly a victim of Reaganomics. I believe they set all the schizophrenics free in '86, or was it '87. We bear you no malice. The eggs are very nice.

—Suckass? Pig dog?

She came to a standstill five feet away, dropped the egg carton and began to pick lint off her cardigan, preoccupied.

—See Ken? A kind word does the trick.

—Anyways we can defend ourselves, said Ken. —Mother's little helper, and with a quick flash of teeth he pulled a corkscrew from the greasy folds of his jacket.

—Where did you get that Ken, said Decetes.

—Found it . . . .

They left the bag lady combing her hair with a plastic fork.

—What else have you found, Ken?

—I gotta locker with some stuff, gotta .22 but that's a girlie gun and I got a good Ruger and some blades.

In the pawn shop Decetes proffered his coinage and was told it would fetch the measly ransom of forty dollars. —1921, take a gander at that, said Decetes. —1914, First World War mint here. These things are worth more than forty bucks.

The woman shook her head and took a phone call.

Ken was looking at knives, the display case open behind Decetes, unsheathing them and holding the glinting blades up to the light. —Cool it there Ken you're not Geronimo, said Decetes.

—Lookit this, CASE V-44, said Ken. —You gotcher folding machetes here too, you gotcher Bowies, gotcher Abalone shell handle here, beautiful blade see this? It's Damascus steel. Practically hard as a diamond. Mokume dagger! Nickel damascus, yeah. She's a beaut. This is a Fairbairn-Sikes Decetes! Custom-made!

—Know your knives Ken, I'll give you that. All right, I'll take the forty. Let's get out of here Ken.

On the sidewalk Ken revealed a small folding knife he had slipped into his pants.

—A little combat folder Decetes. See this? The handle's genuine stag.

Due to her bereavement, he would have to proceed with caution. He would be her pillar, her staunch support, rock of Gibraltar in this time of need. When the mourning was complete, she would give of herself.

There were, of course, habits he would have to break. The filthy cigarettes, the short skirts, the cavalier hygiene, all that would have to be addressed, but gently, in his own sweet time. He could stand at the graveside with her, a firm hand on her shoulder. Make her into a virgin again. Mary Magdalene, beautiful penitent whore. He would reform her. Only for him.

Above her. Bites of a salty peach. Fruit of the tree. Slurping the peach, filthy but scrumptious. Everything in its place. Worship and sacrament. Wild and rhythmic at first, then later with their heads bowed upright beams of light. Back and forth in perpetuity. Horizontal and vertical, first the earth then the air. By day a great house of rectitude, with slurping at night. Something to atone for. Not nothing as now. No soft unwilling organs. No small pink turtle, shrinking at the sight. Rather a rearing snake. Python unleashed! The raw muscle. Patrician with her beside him, other lesser men wanting, slim-erect-an-idol, her blond lovely yet humbled by his word, eyes widened by the eagles in their might. By night a chastised beggar moaning for the rod.

—How is Barbara today? Has she recovered?

—Yes!—thank you Bucella.

His domestic situation was an impediment, yes. He would have to clean house. Ring out the old, ring in the new. The rotten vessels cast to the rocks.

Her hair spread out around her face like a halo of golden fire.

—What about that blue gnome?

—Excuse me?

—The garden gnome she stole. It's sitting in my kitchen.

—Surely the object has no intrinsic value.

—But it belongs to someone.

—We can discuss it later Bucella. I have work to do.

3:01

Alice, on break, sat smoking and drinking her coffee on a concrete bench beside a flowering palm next to the building. It was a placid day, traffic rushing like a steady river behind the spiky trees. She watched the smoke rise and disperse. When she was sixteen she had invented punishments for Ray and spun them out into epics. He had been lectured by stern judges, kicked by thugs, mocked and jeered at by children.

But none of this had ever happened.

Beside her the bench was vacant. Ray was not sitting there; he was not sitting anywhere. What did gone mean?

One summer she'd built castles out of creek silt, buttressed by twigs and ringed with moats. Crayfish got to be the alligators of the moats, with pale green bodies and red claws. She trapped them there and watched their stalks of eyes brush against the moat walls. When dusk fell she collapsed the walls and let them into the stream again. Back then she had thought all she wanted was to live on the coast, the end of earth and beginning of ocean, where men could not walk. In water her small legs could do as much as Ray's big ones. It was an endless dream of blue.

But the tall ships were gone, and the most she got was a syringe in her foot or a day cruise out to Catalina with tourists and sunscreen. Once on a windless Sunday she had driven up to Malibu and stood on the lip of a cliff at Pepperdine, and then she saw the blue. But its peacefulness was an illusion; this was the land of no escape. The sea was a free-for-all, real estate with no title. Shrimpers with their snares cast like gray wings, industry afloat with drift nets a hundred miles long. Going and gone the fish, going gone the great slow giants of the deep, the living coral reefs. Give them time, and they all would be gone.

Honey mama's gotta go to work. You jist call 911 fe comes round agin. You got that sweetie, 9,1,1.

3:10

—I never stoled a camcorder before, said Ken, gnawing on a cord of beef jerky. —Electronics is hard.

—Strategy Ken, it's all strategy, said Decetes reassuringly. —And make it digital. We're going to make a movie.

—After that you gonna set me up with July: Jezebel?

—All in good time. You will have your dream date Ken, just leave it to beaver.

—You talk to the sales guy okay Decetes? So he doesn't watch me.

—Sure Ken. We're on your turf here my son. Let me hold your little knife for you.

Ken hauled the knife out of his grimy athletic sock, handed it over and swaggered through the sliding doors. Decetes stashed the blade in his pocket and followed.

—If something goes wrong Ken, just start running. Rendezvous behind the parking structure in the alley at six p.m. I'll be right behind you all the time Ken, moral support. I will distract the employees. But remember Ken, this is no petty shoplifting caper. This is the glorious beginning of the last crusade.

Bucella clicked her mouse and exited SAS. She was too distracted to run a multivariate regression. She was a Sister of Charity, tending the Infirm and Deranged with no Reward. She was surrounded by the Profane, but walked through it with her head held High. Catherine of Siena took a vow of Virginity, Mary of Oignies helped Lepers. And hardly anyone appreciated them either, before they were dead.

In her whole life she'd never done anything mean to anyone, except maybe in fifth grade when she killed a frog by mistake. However frogs apparently had no Souls, although the girl who brought it in to show and tell did have a Soul. Plus, for the rest of the year after that she gave the girl her snackfood at Recess, be it celery with peanut butter or oatmeal cookies. One week, when she had no snacks, she gave the girl five pennies from her piggybank, one penny every day. Dean had found out she broke her piggybank for the purpose and stashed the money in a jar. He stole the jar and took the rest of the pennies to buy firecrackers. Then he burned down a Historical Oak.

They suspended him after that, but it didn't bring her pennies back.

Phillip Kreuz never even apologized for his wife. That mentally challenged Felon. Gnome stealer and Vomitus Maximus. He had borrowed her staple remover three weeks ago and never gave it back. Now she was going to get it. She pushed her swivel chair back and walked to his desk, approaching him from behind. He was bent over, a paper smoothed across his knees.

She reached out a hand to tap him smartly on the shoulder but then withdrew it fast before it touched. *We are twinned—*
Lordy God!

3:40

—Please, you have to come down here, you have to come, wailed Riva. Alice had returned to her desk to find the phone ringing yet again. —Jerry's out to lunch and there's no one else!

—Just tell me what happened, said Alice. —Slow down and tell me what happened.

—It's the police, said Riva. —I gave them the description and they called back and said there was, there . . . .

—What was there, said Alice. —I'm listening. Go on.

—They say there's a girl who meets her description . . . .

—Yes?

—She's, it's a dead girl. They say I have to go to the morgue and identify—what—

—Stay there, said Alice. —Oh. Where is there?

3:52

He would keep her in his sights. She was inclined to be free-wheeling, disregarding her own safety at the drop of a hat. For now. Before the new regime.

Fortunately he had parked his rental on the street, and could follow her easily. He was not surprised to learn that she drove as erratically as she behaved. It was all he could do to stay close without violating traffic regulations, which had after all been promulgated for the sake of collective welfare. He made a mental note to remind her of this at an appropriate time. Reckless driving was a crime like any other. He stopped at a red light. She was two cars ahead. A Mexican stood on the median, hawking oranges and grapes. Phillip rolled down his window.

—Orange orange? Three-dollar bag?

—Please be advised that I am planning to report you to the proper authorities, said Phillip sternly. Patrician. The eagles spread their wings. —Do you possess a vending permit?

—Grape one dollar bag señor, extra cheap.

—Obviously you do not. Have those fruits been checked for pesticide residue and parasites?

—Real cheap, orange yust three dollars, said the man, and leaned down close to Phillip's head at the window, holding out a bag. His teeth were blackened and he smelled. Phillip quickly retracted his head. The proximity could be dangerous. A smell signaled molecules entering his nasal passages. They might well be molecules of disease.

—Are you an illegal alien? If necessary, I will telephone the Immigration and Naturalization Service. I am a taxpayer, unlike yourself. That fruit may constitute a hazard to public health. I,N,S. Do you hear me? INS!

—Don't try to scare me you cheap asshole, said the man with no trace of an accent. —I'm as American as apple pie.

Good gracious. Thankfully the light had turned green. As Phillip pulled away a bag of oranges smashed across the side of his face. His glasses fell. Grappling to hook them on his ear again, he lost his grip on the wheel and narrowly missed the bumper ahead as he swerved.

4:02

Bucella hid in the bathroom, having Palpitations. He had probably stolen the letter right out of the envelope on Ernest's desk. Marked PRIVATE INTEROFFICE MAIL. He could be laughing and mocking her this very second. Why did he do it? She just tried to be a good hostess and friendly coworker. His wife desecrated her house when it was just steam-cleaned, costing two hundred dollars, and then he read her private correspondence. Even the saints had been known to cry out against their Attackers. He was sitting there right now laughing, rubbing his hands and chortling.

It was after lunch hour, and anyway she knew for a fact that he never went home for lunch. He brought tuna sandwiches in foil or soup in a Tupperware container.

She pushed her chair back on its rollers and grabbed the key to the Budget Rent-a-Car Buick. Then she looked on her list of employee home numbers and wrote down his address on a Post-It.

An eye for an eye.

16:19

—They found her last night! said Riva.

She was chafing her wrists, flushed, and had bit into her bottom lip until it bled. Walking beside her Alice put an arm around her shoulders, stared down at the linoleum unfurling itself beneath them. A morgue technician strode ahead. Alice noted his white rubber-soled shoes: vinyl nurse's shoes with patterns of perforated dots.

—They said a knife! She was a mathematics gifted. My little girl. Gifted!

—Don't think about that right now, said Alice gently.

—Right through here ladies.

The room was large and clean. They stood behind him waiting. He pulled back a curtain. Alice saw Riva's chin shake. A covered form on a gurney. Riva balled her hands into fists.

—Whopper and fries, called another technician over his shoulder as he sped out the double doors.

—Are you ready ma'am?

Alice's wrist was squeezed. She was an impostor, a stand-in. She would hunt down the absentee husband and flog him to within an inch of his life. The sheet was pulled back. A small brown head, face still.

—It's a—it's a *black* person!

Riva released Alice's wrist to clap her hands.

—This is a little *black* girl!

Alice felt the muscles of her cheeks loosen. There was an obscenity in it, an obscene freedom.

—She's not it. It's not her!

Riva was shaking her head, with a smile that stretched her lips too far. Alice bent over the small head. A slight dent in the skin beside the nose. It looked like a scar from chicken-pox. The face seemed softer than felt.

—I'm sorry, it must—an unacceptable, uh, error—

—My baby's not dead!

—I'm very sorry, stuttered the technician, —What a ridiculous—I just came on, I don't—do you know who called you? Jesus!

He snapped the sheet back up with a jerk of his wrist.

—It's okay, it's just fine, it's not her! babbled Riva, smiling giddily. Stupid with relief.

—Let's go please, said Alice.

4:26

She finished calculating his total surface area. Sure Mr. Alan was skinny, but he was also tall. She sat down on the bedroom floor, spread the white sheet out on the carpet and began to cut it into strips.

In *Cleopatra Empress of the Nile* there were slaves. They built the pyramids with their bare hands. In those days they didn't have bulldozers but it didn't matter because they had slaves.

Jonah T. would have made a good slave. He lifted free weights four hours a day and his room was full of barbells, gold, black and silver ones, plus Jonah T. had all these trophies on shelves he built himself. The trophies were for javelin, shotput and junior bodybuilding competitions. Every time she went into Jonah T.'s room, no matter how many times she'd already seen it, he showed her all the trophies again like it was some big deal, not saying much but just leaning against the shelf and nodding his head like he was hot shit, when they were just a bunch of plastic crap painted to look like brass. Once she flicked the paint off with a fingernail and there was cheap white plastic underneath.

Liza B. said he cut class to buy steroids from some guy in Tijuana. Guys like Jonah T. probably wouldn't mind being slaves as long as they got trophies for it to show girls in their room. Most Rocks Lifted in L.A. County in the year 2004.

She knew where there was a pyramid. It was far away in Las Vegas. She saw it in a movie on Cinemax. It even had that big lion in front of it, the Spinks. Like in Egypt. She would have to drive him there and it could take a long time, but it was worth it. Once she saw a movie called *The Mummy Walks*. That was on Cinemax too, before her mother cancelled it because of bad influence. Anyway *The Mummy Walks* wasn't scary just dumb. The special effects looked homemade.

She lifted his left leg, holding it by the bony ankle, and smeared Krazy Glue like Mike Lamota once sniffed in Shop till his nose bled. She had got it from Mr. Alan's kitchen closet. It would keep the strips of cotton from unwinding. If Mr. Alan was a mummy he could live forever. The curse would be lifted one day and he would rise from the tomb, not scary but just a little dumb like regular people could be.

If she did this she was done and clear and home free.

—It's okay Mr. Alan. See Mr. Alan, it's okay.

4:38

Approaching the Kreuzes' apartment she saw two workmen coming out the front door, rolling something between them. It was a stroke of luck. The martyrs would be avenged! She would anyway, and she stood for all of them. She walked boldly and with confidence like she was supposed to be there.

—Hello.

—You the lady of the house?

They were pulling and pushing a metal cart with a large crate on it.

—Yes I am, said Bucella.

—All yours then.

They rolled it down to the sidewalk and the second one waved at her casually as she slipped in the front door and closed it. The Kreuz apartment was spotless. Clearly they kept their own place spic-'n-span, and went elsewhere to vomit.

She saw a list stuck to the refrigerator.

1. *Lightbulbs 40-watt not 60. Remember this time Barbara!*
2. *1% Acidophilus Milk. Expiration date!*
3. *3-4 p.m. Spiritual Health!*

Next to the phone was a red Sharpie marker. She picked it up and went back to the front door and opened it just enough to get her arm out. They hadn't noticed CHI and STER so they wouldn't connect it with her. She craned her neck around the doorjamb, saw the coast was clear and quickly scribbled in big block letters THIEF!!! Without further Ado.

To paint it over wouldn't cost two hundred dollars but maybe fifteen or twenty. She shut the door and went back to the kitchen, where she unplugged the fridge for good measure. Hopefully it contained a hundred and eighty dollars' worth of perishables. She was victorious! Sure it wasn't exactly Turn the Other Cheek, but sometimes it couldn't be. Everyone was a sinner anyway, etc.

Then she walked back through the living room into the hall, gazing at Inspirational Plaques on the walls. They were not embroidered but printed sternly. *We must have trials and self-denials, until all error is destroyed. —Mary Baker Eddy, 1875.* He had probably coerced the Challenged Felon into stealing the gnome. He was probably a Kleptomaniac.

She tried one door, but it revealed a closet lined with cleaning agents. Comet, Formula 409, Lysol, Anti-Bacterial Soap, Woolite Spot & Stain, Windex, Pine Sol, Arm & Hammer. She closed the door and tried another. It was their bedroom. Twin beds, neatly made. Each had an identical alarm clock beside it and an identical lamp. There was only one difference: across the pillow of one bed lay a stuffed animal. It was a floppy-eared dog with a ribbon around its neck and a heart pendant hanging from the ribbon. On the pendant were the words *Arf Arf I Wuv Oo.* Even the dog was mentally challenged. She picked it up, opened the window and threw it out.

Finally she opened the last door off the hall. Lordy God! Buck Naked, sitting strapped to the toilet with silver tape over her mouth, was the Retard herself. Bucella screamed.

4:44

—Young man, I would like to test-drive your top-of-the-line wide-screen TV. I have a palsy in my right hand. You will have to man the controls for me, if you would be so good.

The salesperson was slow-moving and bovine. His eyes were dulled with boredom.

—Uh okay. I guess. This one here's the biggest, that what you want?

—I was looking for something a little larger, but that will have to do I suppose. What is the retail price?

Out of the corner of his eye he caught sight of Ken, grazing placidly amongst the video equipment. His head could barely be seen over the shelf.

—$1999. Lemme go get a DVD to pop in there.

And the meek shall inherit the earth.

—You wanna screen *E.T.* or *Apocalypse Now?*

4:52

She had entered the building marked CORONER some time ago, but had still not emerged. Phillip remained at the wheel of the rental, parked across the street, watching the building's doors. He tapped a march beat on the steering wheel, which he had sterilized cautiously with a Handiwipe before he initiated epidermal contact. He noticed a smear on the gunmetal matte of the dashboard. It was located next to the odometer, and yellow-white in color. A weaker man might be drawn to speculate on its origin or properties, but Phillip refused. He would not look at it. That way lay abomination.

The doors of the Coroner's building could disgorge his quarry at any moment. She had left the office soon after she was informed of her father's demise; probably she had come here to identify his remains. She would be in a weakened state when she came out again. His presence would be required to soothe her.

Her letter had been unexpected, he had to concede. She hid her devotion well. Possibly the personal tragedy would strip her of her false confidence, her indifferent facade.

She wanted to be stripped. That was clear.

4:55

—Goodness me, said Bucella. —These *are* tight.

She had managed to peel the tape off the mouth and was at work on the tape that had Barbara's feet trussed to the base of the toilet. Meanwhile the patient sat there slack-jawed. She held a towel up to her chest, which Bucella had handed her quickly from a rack on the wall. She obviously failed to understand its purpose however, since she kept letting it slip off her lap, and when it did Bucella saw her Good Gracious. —I came over to, um, check up on you after last night, she told her as she picked at a gummy edge. It was a lie but only a white one. —The door was wide open. Didn't you hear me calling?

—They took Bronco Bill, said Barbara in a monotone.

—A large crate was removed, I noticed that, said Bucella. One strip of tape peeled free, but there were many more. Scissors would do the trick. —Where are the scissors? she asked Barbara.

—I heard them take Bronco Bill. He did this so I couldn't stop them.

—Who taped you? asked Bucella. —*Phillip*? He taped you to the toilet? Your own husband?

—He taped me so they could take Bronco Bill.

—Bronco Bill, said Bucella. —A pet? You bought a dog?

—Bronco Bill, said Barbara, shaking her head slowly. —Fun in your home, and good for parties.

—Inhumane, said Bucella, fuming. —They carted your dog off in a box with no holes. I will call the ASPCA. But where are the scissors?

—Scissors? asked Barbara dreamily. Clearly Bucella would have to locate them herself.

—Stay right there, I'll be back.

—No riding of Bronco Bill, murmured Barbara behind her.

For the mentally Deficient, it was obviously difficult to distinguish between dogs and horses. Dog-loving was this woman's hobby. She had talked about it throughout dinner and on her pillow was Arf Arf the Challenged Spaniel. Bucella went outside, bent down and picked up the fluffy pooch from the sidewalk. Possibly it would serve to console the woman for the loss of her real pet.

5:02

Decetes had time to kill before his appointment with Ken. Passing storefronts and bicycle racks, stunted shrubs in concrete blocks and multiple-personality war amputees riddled with sores and reeking of piss, he liberated a knapsack from a chair on a restaurant patio. Its contents were exposed during a rapid search in a men's room. They included a textbook entitled *Economics: The Science of Common Sense*, a pink lipstick, a keychain featuring a rubber Pokémon, and a bulging wallet. Hosanna in the highest.

Decetes was pleased with the driver's license. *Deborah Louise Grossman*, it said, but the round-lettered signature read *Debbie*. He was gratified to note that the name on Debbie's American Express card was not Deborah Louise Grossman but Leon B. Grossman.

Leon B. entered an upscale bar and signed his name with a flourish when the bar tab was presented. Four whiskey sours and a plate of breaded scampi. Catch as catch can. The youthful must be tutored in the rigid regulations of Darwinism, or they would never know the satiation of a fresh kill. Weaker, small-bodied animals were commonly left to scavenge through heaps of old carrion, to find their meager nourishment in the leavings of the strong. Once again, he, Dean Decetes, had rendered a service. He was an educator as well as an ironclad man of action.

Deborah Louise Grossman would not remain Debbie for long.

5:09

—You should go home and rest now, said Alice. —Your daughter will come back. Teenagers go off on their own. Asserting independence. It's only normal.

—She's having relations, said Riva. —With boys.

—Count your blessings, said Alice.

—It's that school. They teach them Sex Ed and how to use a diaphragm. I found one in her room.

—I'm sorry but I'm tired, said Alice. —I have to go. Don't worry about the clothes. You can keep them.

5:11

He watched her step into her vehicle and slam the door. Only a silhouette was visible. She sat there with her head bent. Phillip sympathized. It was always unpleasant to view the remains of a parent.

His own father had gone to his reward from a nursing home in Marina del Rey. Phillip had visited him most punctiliously, once every two months on Saturday mornings from nine until 10:15. It was before he met Barbara the wolf in sheep's clothing, that dark day in Vons.

The elder Mr. Kreuz disappeared during seniors bingo and could not be located by the attendants. Since he suffered from Alzheimer's they feared he had wandered into traffic or toppled into a canal. Finally, however, they found him under his cot, in a fetal position, clutching a woman's old bedroom slipper. He was deceased of a heart attack.

She edged out of her parallel parking slot, looking over her shoulder. He turned the key in the ignition.

5:15

Barbara, still naked as the day she was born, had wandered into her kitchen and was standing in front of the open refrigerator, dazed. Either she was in shock or her subnormal mental abilities rendered her immune to certain stimuli. Bucella felt guilty. It was becoming more and more obvious that the poor woman was a Victim of her arch-criminal Spouse. Special people had great faith in God.

—Goodness, your refrigerator seems to be unplugged, said Bucella —I'll just plug it in for you. There we go.

—I can't be the best possible me, muttered Barbara as she dropped an egg into the sink.

—Excuse me, ventured Bucella, approaching with averted eyes. —I don't mean to pry, but I suspect this may be an abuse situation. A husband is not supposed to tape his wife to the toilet. Phillip may not want you to have a pet but that is no excuse for domestic aggression. I'm sure you did not enjoy having that electrical tape ripped from your mouth. I understand. I come from a broken home myself.

—I wanted to ride Bronco Bill, said Barbara. —Good for abs.

—Of course you did, said Bucella.

It would serve no clear purpose to disabuse her of the notion that dogs could be ridden like ponies. Possibly she had loved horses as a girl, and was still holding fast to her Dream. Her mother had probably not let her ride a horse. Mentals and equestrians did not go hand in hand.

—Phillip told you to steal that garden gnome, didn't he?

—He said Mind of Christ. . . .

—I'll bet he did. I hate to break it to you but your husband is a thief. Come on, I'll help you get dressed. We're going to teach him a lesson.

5:41

Decetes strode out of Korean Massage with a spring in his step. They took credit cards, and Leon B. was a man with chronic muscle fatigue. The little geisha had no tits, but she could deal out handjobs with the best of them. Leon B. would make a whirlwind tour tonight, before Debbie had time to blow the whistle. Sharper than a serpent's tooth, to have a thankless child, but Leon B. would forgive her in time. He could hit every Handjob Haven in town before dawn. By sunrise he'd be dry as a bone.

There was a payphone not twenty paces ahead. He clutched the Classifieds lovingly to his chest. Ho! A man stood in front of him, big as a house and black as the ace of spades.

—Speak of the devil. You remember me bud? From Sizzler?

—Can't place the name but the face is familiar, lied Decetes, attempting a sidestep. Leon B. protected his plastic assets.

—You don't remember me now, you'll remember me soon, said the leviathan. —*Boy.*

5:49

Alice had decided without deciding, after the dead girl. She was headed for the bar, dark and enclosed. The dark was so lovable! No measuring sticks, no unsightly rashes. Fear slid away, and in its place there was the roaring instinct of release. Embarrassment left, time stopped threatening, and the world lost all its sharp teeth. The world was toothless and velvet.

Yep, drown her sorrows like puppies in a bag, on the bed of a slow-flowing river. No houses, trees, cars, airplanes. Only warm nothing, where you went when you died.

Still, over the bones and moss a breeze drifted. One day she'd know what to do and how to do it. Possessed by the spirit of victory, in the turn of a second, she would watch the fractured splinters of her will fuse again, a perfect sphere of resolve. It would illuminate her landscape like the noonday sun.

Until then, and against the chance it never would, have a drink.

She slowed to a stop at a red light.

—Orange three dollar, grape super-cheap.

—Are they seedless?

—No seeds señorita, grape one dollar super deal.

—Here. Thank you.

She parked a few blocks away from The Quiet Man. Walking always provided the illusion of progress: when she walked she was going somewhere, even if she wasn't. She ate from her bag of grapes as she strolled, felt the warm air on her shoulders and smiled. *Strolling*. She was strolling, as though delighted at the privilege. Young, she used to peel each grape before she ate it, careful not to make dents in the pulp with her fingernails. She said to herself that they were the tender eyeballs of plants. They had to be kept whole until the very last moment.

When she'd eaten half the bag she ducked into a corner payphone and dialed the office.

—Ernie it's Alice. I'm having a bad day. Long story, but I was just at the morgue with a little dead girl and a woman who was happy to see her.

—Are you kidding? You poor dear! Someone you knew?

—No. I didn't know her.

—Still . . . listen, sweetie, there's no one here anyway. I'm a rat on a sinking ship. Relax. Drink some Lemon Zinger, do a peel-off facial mask. Meditate.

—Thanks Ernie. I'll do that. I'll do something.

—So what did you think of the dress?

—I think you look better in A-lines.

—I knew it. The ruffles were too much. I looked like a wedding cake. Just say it, you won't hurt my feelings. Say Ernie, you looked like a wedding cake. Someone should put you in a freezer for twenty-five years and take you out for the Silver Anniversary. Come on. Hurt me.

—Ernie, you looked like a wedding cake. But you danced like Carmen Miranda.

—You are so brutally honest.

—Hold on. I think I see someone I know.

Unbelievable, almost. Slithering along the pavement like a snake, on his stomach, was Bucella's drunken brother.

Alice stared.

—It's Bucella's brother. You remember? The drunken pornographer who kept falling down at Thanksgiving? He's lying on the sidewalk in front of me. Right now. He seems to be pulling himself along by his chin.

—That poor man.

—Ernie he's a piece of human flotsam. The other night he leapt on top of me at a party and had a hard-on the size of a Blutwurst. I'll see you tomorrow.

She hung up and approached.

—Excuse me. Do you need some help?

He rolled over onto his back and gazed at her. His face was like a raw slab of beef, washed-out blue eyes glistening between bloodied flaps.

—You're hurt. Let's get you onto the bench.

—You have fine breasts, for a Samaritan.

—Don't look a gift horse in the mouth. Take my hand. Upsy daisy.

She hoisted him and guided him to the bench with an arm around his waist. He limped, and as she bent to sit him down he trailed the back of one arm mournfully across her pelvis.

—You're a scumbag, but you already knew that. So what happened? Been doing more falling down lately?

—Most Samaritans are not known for their secondary sexual characteristics, he said, licking blood and dirt off his upper lip. He adjusted himself with a casual hand on his fly.
—Take Mother Teresa, for instance, though I was never a fan

of hers myself. It might be hypothesized that Samaritanism is inversely proportionate to sex appeal. Madam, you are a notable exception.

—What a schmuck, said Alice. —Do you even remember me? I work with your sister. My name is Alice.

—I am Leon B. Grossman, said the drunk. —Might I interest you in a small charitable act of fellatio?

—Jesus, said Alice. —If that's all, I think I'll be on my way.

6:07

Decetes watched her stroll past the facades of commerce. Lenscrafters, All American Burger. They had passed like ships in the night. In time she would worship at the altar of his lingam just like the rest. Time was his trump card. The most recent beating had been a mild one, but in the hurly burly he had become fatigued. He patted his pocket. Yes, he still had the plastic of Leon B. Grossman. It would be a rich, fulfilling evening.

And Ken was waiting in the wings even now with the movie machine. It would make them immortal. Ken less so than Decetes, of course. Decetes would lie patiently until his strength returned, meditative as the Buddha.

The wood of his bench was painted dark green, the color of primeval forests fast disappearing. Here, at the bus stop, they were remembered in latex-based acrylic. He for one would not protest. Tranquility. A tree falls. Makes no sound. Still, Ken would not wait forever. Decetes stood up slowly.

6:11

Mr. Alan was ready. The bedroom smelled like Krazy Glue. Now she had to pick up her mother's car to drive him to the Spinks. It was parked like nine blocks away.

She grabbed the keys off the dresser and went out.

6:14

—Ladies and Grunts, attention please. I'm starting the service.

—Hear hear!

—Thanks.

The biker cleared his throat.

—Jack the Sailor's life was no walk in the park. He was hatched about twelve years ago, in an open-air market in San José, Costa Rica. In the weeks and months after his entrance into this world Jack the Sailor was subjected to much hardship and suffering.

—Hardship!

—Suffering!

—At the age of six months he was shipped from Costa Rica to Miami on a banana boat. During the voyage many of his associates passed away, some of trauma, some of thirst, and others of starvation and disease. But Jack the Sailor was a survivor.

—What the hell is this? whispered Alice to the bartender. Patrons were grouped in a semicircle around the grizzled motorcyclist she'd known. He stood near the back of the bar, reading slowly off a sheet of crumpled paper. There was a wreath nailed to the wall behind him, and in the middle of a table sat a shoebox inscribed with the slogan *Just Do It*.

—Memorial, said the bartender.

—For whom? Don't tell me it's that bird?

—Macaw. Jack the Sailor.

—How did he—?

—Murdered.

—Jack was always very precocious. He said his first words in a pet shop in Orlando, where he resided following his stay in Palm Beach. I didn't know him then, but I heard from his previous owner what the words were. One sunny day, not five nautical miles from Disneyworld, Jack ruffled his wingfeathers, spread his tailfeathers and said, "Hi. I'm looking for a gerbil."

—Jesus, said Alice. —It never rains but it pours. Vodka tonic please.

CHAPTER THE SEVENTH

Burials take place; a sheep is shorn; the Innocent is set free;
and an Honest Man is robbed of his Freedom

When she parked her car, he had been forced to leave his own behind and follow her at a distance of half a block. After assisting the transient on the sidewalk, she had disappeared into a bar. Now he was relegated to the cement expanse of a Toyota dealership, where he stood perspiring in the gray, smog-laden twilight. Ground-level ozone was both un-hygienic and hazardous to his respiratory welfare: insofar, of course, as he permitted it to be. If he were not acutely aware of the risks presented by cuticle infection, he would be biting his nails. She had entered the bar, surely, in an act of provocative abandon; she wanted to be told what to do, forcibly restrained from the self-immolation of vice. She wished to compel him to take a firm hand. And yet such a calculation would suggest she was aware of his presence.

—May I help you sir?

—No, said Phillip. —Please leave me alone.

—Were you looking for something sporty, or a family vehicle?

—Nothing, said Phillip. —I already have a car.

—We have a very affordable two-door in the $17,000 range.

—I am not, I repeat not in the market for an automobile.

—With only $2,000 down, our customers have the benefit of an unbeatable 100,000-mile warranty.

6:27

He would reclaim what was rightfully his. If necessary, he would employ force. Alan H. might be a slave-driver at HQ, but in his own home he would be at a distinct disadvantage. He would soon be persuaded.

—Wait for you here?

—Yes Ken. Guard the camcorder Ken, and guard it with your life.

If he remembered correctly from the confidential personnel files, Alan H. lived on the second floor. He made his way slowly up the outdoor stairs, favoring his right foot, which had been trod upon by the giant from Sizzler. It was a split-level Italianate villa with a tile roof. Alan H. did not stint on his comfort.

The door was heavy wood, unpainted, with a wrought-iron window grille. Decetes knocked once forcefully, then again.

No answer.

—Hey Decetes!

Turning swiftly to reprimand Ken for the intrusion, he felt a pang shoot up his right leg. His ankle buckled and he collapsed against the door, shoulder cracking. Swords and plowshares!

The door pushed open and he staggered in and fell.

—You okay Decetes?

—Ken, I would be alone.

—Here Decetes, grab onto my arm.

—Anybody home? I will rest a moment on the couch Ken.

—Nice place. . . .

Ken forged a path into the interior, shuffling through the kitchen while Decetes nursed his leg. The living room was well-appointed, he was willing to concede. Its ceilings bespoke cathedrals, its walls museums. There was a stark contrast between Alan H.'s austere art objects and the fluffy bric-à-brac with which Bucella lined her nest.

—Hey Decetes! Wow Decetes! You gotta see this!

6:30

Barbara was helping herself to Planter's Peanuts. She ate like a pig, but she could hardly be blamed.

—You're safe here. We'll have dinner and you can stay for the night. Your husband has to learn he can't go taping you to plumbing willy-nilly. Plus his thieving has to be nipped in the bud. That should be a condition if you two make up. I will not tell our employer yet, but I may have to if the thieving continues. We have an honor code. You can sleep here tonight. My brother comes home late when he comes home at all. You'll take his couch. It folds out. He can just sleep on the floor.

When Bucella came back from the bathroom Barbara had found one of Dean's Publications and was gaping at the centerfold.

—Put that away! It belongs to my brother, snapped Bucella, snatching the rag out of Barbara's limp hands. Mentals were notorious for their indecent interest in Adult

Matters. This was why Barbara had shed her clothing so quickly under the influence of Alcohol. She must be taught to restrain herself. It was embarrassing. —He is the black sheep of the family.

—Naked ladies.

—Yes, they are naked. But we're not interested in them.

6:39

—My personal favorite is the Corolla, here on your left. Optimal gas mileage, one of the top ratings for service in Consumer Reports, smooth handling and a luxury feel.

Phillip had reached the end of his rope. He stepped onto the sidewalk and crossed the street.

6:41

—Len, two drafts.

—A draft and one Tequila chaser.

They were all converging at the bar. The biker, at her elbow, set his shoebox on the counter. He smelled of sweat.

—'Preciate you being here, he said. —Hardly knew him.

—He swore at me a few times, said Alice.

—Beaten to death, said the biker. —Random violence.

—I know it well, said Alice. —Was it something he said?

—Lemme get your drink, said the biker.

—That's not necessary, said Alice.

—Least I can do, said the biker. —Gimme a break here. Sorry for that message on your machine. It was outta line.

—Alice!

She turned to see Phillip Kreuz standing behind her, in coat and tie. Fish out of water. He had his hands on his hips.

—Phil! I didn't know you went to bars! Shouldn't you be at work?

—Alice I know what you want.

—That makes one of us Phil. A drink?

—I mean it Alice. Come with me. We will leave.

—Who the fuck is this guy?

—A coworker of mine. Is something wrong Phil?

—Alice I know your father is deceased but grief is not a license for debauchery or sins of the flesh.

—Sins? This guy's pissing me off. She's with me, okay guy?

—I'll handle this. No one's sinning Phil, at least no more than usual. I took half a sick day. Don't worry about me. I'll see you tomorrow. I promise I'll make it to work alive.

—Alice that is not the point. A place like this is inappropriate.

—Listen guy, I understand you work with Alice here but what she does on her sick days is none of your business.

—This individual is not the kind you should associate with. He is a lower-class individual. Riff raff off the street.

—Okay. This fucker is asking for it.

—Phil, I appreciate your concern but now is not the time for a socioeconomic discussion.

He leaned toward her urgently.

—Alice, I received your communication.

—My—?

—I know the lay of the land. You asked for my protection. Now come with me and leave this den of iniquity behind. Your father's death was a blow, I realize that, but you cannot let it affect your moral judgment. The person beside you is gutter trash. You could catch something.

—That's it. Get the fuck out of her face.

6:49

—Ken my boy, it would appear to be a corpse. There cannot be any doubt.

—Decetes how come there's holes for the mouth and nose but not the eyes?

Decetes leaned over the bed once more and peered into the gauze-wrapped face. It was certainly Alan H. Thin lips, thin arms. And he had been mummified.

—It's like a bodycast Decetes. Like in the movies.

—This is not a cast Ken. It is the sheets. He is wrapped in torn sheets.

It was not Decetes's place to question the mysterious workings of providence. She was ever his mistress.

—You grab his shoulders Ken, I'll get the ankles. We're taking this lad on his final vacation.

7:02

Omigod he was gone. There was a dent in the mattress where he'd been, but he was gone. *The Mummy Walks*. She stood in the bedroom door staring, and then checked under the bed. In the closet. In the bathroom.

—Mr. Alan?

If he got up and walked away it meant he was okay. Okay!

She'd just went crazy and imagined everything. He probably gave her drugs last night in the Dr. Pepper and made her see hallucinations this whole time. Peyote or maybe it was some really bad acid. After all he was definitely sicko. And now the drugs had worn off.

She jumped up and down. Happy.

—He's just fine there Ken, a Dumpster is better than a coffin. Sturdier Ken, and abundant fresh air. I have a few calls to make Ken, wouldn't want them to find him before the cat's out of the bag.

They made their way to a payphone on Wilshire, leaving the Dumpster behind. Decetes fingered his pocket with its new wad of cash. Alan H. had apparently not trusted banks.

—Go to the store there on the corner Ken, here's some money. I am in some pain Ken. Get me a pack of Marlboros. If you would be so kind.

With Ken safely out of the way Decetes dropped a quarter in the slot and called HQ. He disguised his voice craftily, by means of a plastic bag for static.

—This is Alan. Won't be in for a couple of weeks, checked into rehab. Some people did an intervention. In the meantime I'm rehiring Dean Decetes. He can act as editor in my absence. Don't question this, I realize it's a stretch, but Decetes does know the ropes. I'll call again in a week.

He hung up quickly. Ken was approaching with two cigarette packs.

—Here Decetes, they had a special two for one deal.

—A place I know Ken, called Korean Massage. I have associates there. It will be on the house Ken. My treat. A reward for your first day of service. And that is only the beginning Ken. Tonight we will paint the town red.

—Ladies from the magazine? July: Jezebel?

—These ladies, Ken, are free agents.

—But how about July: Jezebel?

—You will meet her in time. Jezebel has a busy schedule. Her dance card is full Ken, more often than not.

—But when Decetes? When?

—Perhaps tomorrow Ken, we'll see. Here we go my boy, right here. I will escort you inside.

7:17

—Take your hands off me, Phillip cried indignantly, but they jostled him out the door and sent him sprawling with a shove. Though his temples were throbbing from the rough handling he righted himself immediately and began the walk to his rental. She was much farther gone than he had expected, enslaved to her vices. The bitch! Humiliation. No, no. Quell the anger. Sin could not be beaten out of her skin, but must be coaxed. Her face and her voice were veritable walls of denial. They denied her pitiful outcry, that pitiful and virtuous outcry made in the silent language of paper. She was afraid to yield, her habits were ingrained, and she disguised her fear with composure. The letter had been a plea for help from a lost woman who was battling her sordid impulses. But he must not give in.

Striding briskly, he took a shortcut through the parking lot of a minimall, distracted by a pain in his neck. Possibly whiplash. He hedged his way between two vehicles and was already past them, on the sidewalk, when he stopped dead and turned. It was the hit-and-run, the purloined Pinto responsible for his Hyundai's destruction. He recognized a rust formation on the hood.

If he waited to confront the driver, in his weakened state, he might be at a disadvantage. He must take steps. But his cell phone was elsewhere.

He approached the car hesitantly and touched the rear bumper. No alarm was activated. It stood to reason. He tried the front door handle on the driver's side. Locked. He walked around to the passenger side. The window was rolled down: about three inches at the top. He hooked his arm in and popped the lock. There might be identity documents in the glove compartment. The culprit could be isolated and punished.

He opened the creaking door gingerly.

—Step away from the vehicle with your arms raised.

Phillip threw up his arms. Colored lights, rotating. Then he was relieved. It was the Los Angeles Police Department.

—Officer! Thank the Lord.

—Keep your hands in the air. Step away from the vehicle.

A uniformed man approached, touching the bulge on his hip.

—No no, said Phillip impatiently. —You don't—

—Turn around, spread your legs and place your palms far apart on the window.

Phillip complied reluctantly. The man patted his sides and legs, rather abruptly. —I was just about to call. The person who was driving this automobile—

—You are under arrest, said the policeman, and snapped a metal bracelet onto his wrist. Handcuffs, used on common criminals.

—But this isn't my car! I'm not the one who stole it!

—You have the right to remain silent. Anything you say can and will be used against you—

—No no! The person driving this car hit my car! It was a hit-and-run!

—in a court of law. You have the right to an attorney.

—Last night! Let me explain!

—If you cannot afford an attorney, one will be provided for you.

Alice and the biker walked down to the beach. Sand between her toes. He was intent on cremation. Jack the Sailor would go out like a Viking.

Set on a pyre of crumpled newspaper and dead fronds on the sand, the shoebox was slow to ignite. They watched the spikes of palm curl and blacken in the growing dusk. There were colors in the sky, soft strips of purple and yellow over the ocean. Alice stood awkwardly with her arms crossed, eyes fixed on the grubby cardboard. At long last it went up, *Just Do It* to *Do It* and finally *It*. It was a blurry pyre, spits of flame licking the cardboard, sparks drifting over the gently rolling surf.

The biker was crying like a baby. She put out a hand and touched his shoulder.

—I'm gonna scatter his ashes off the pier, said the biker. —Will you come?

He sniffed and blinked as he raked ashes from the sand with his fingers. Progress was slow across the sand: he carried the small pile tenderly, cupped in his palms.

—Ashes to ashes, dust to dust, he said finally, and spread his hands. —Now Jack the Sailor is at one with the sea.

Now Jack the Sailor was a waterborne pollutant, but that didn't make him a lesser soul. Behind them, the pier was ablaze in the setting sun: bumper cars screeched, bells jangled, the ferris wheel rotated sluggishly and teenagers milled at the entrance to the arcade. A man walked past with a tray of fluorescent straws and plastic trolls, suspended by a neck strap. The biker gazed west, eyes brimming.

—So how did he get his name? she asked.

—Because he survived. It's a song, said the biker, and sang. —Jack was every inch a sai-lor, five-and-twenty years at sea.

Alice watched the vendor approach the end of the pier, where a few strides away from them a lone gull pecked at gray, flattened popcorn. The biker wiped his nose with the back of his hand; the vendor took the tray from around his neck and set it carefully on the planking next to the rail. Then he stooped, bent over and ducked between the bars. A light splash. She could barely hear it.

—A vendor just dove off the pier, she said to the biker. He unballed his fists and wiped his eyes with his knuckles.

—The water's shallow, he said. —Families swimming, back near the shore there. In the chemical soup. Mexicans. They're the only people that swim here. Can't read.

—The water's shallow, echoed Alice, leaning over to look down. She saw a faint ring of wake spread out and disappear.

—See, said the biker, starting to cry again. —Call me a fool, I don't care. But I swear, he was my best friend.

7:51

Mr. Alan had a nice watch. It fit onto her ankle. She stuffed her clothes in Mr. Alan's briefcase and wore his big shirt and rolled-up jeans out the door. Going down the steps she skipped. It never happened at all! The whole thing was just one big mirage in the Sahara desert. And now it was over. *89751 divided by 1.82 = 49313.736. Square root of 47813 = 218.66183.* Start all over again with the basic stuff.

Someone's sprinkler was going back and forth, wetting the sidewalk and making it clean.

8:06

—You are missing my point, said Phillip to the desk sergeant. —This vehicle rear-ended my car while it was parked. My car sustained substantial damages!

—Yeah we'll look into it.

They pushed him in front of them, past the desk. Bars!

—My Lord! You can't put me in there!

—Just a holding cell guy. You won't be in here for long.

Phillip struggled, but they had grips of steel. Criminals unbathed and likely unvaccinated stood shoulder to shoulder, exchanging parasites. The bacteria coagulated on their flesh, swam long and whip-tailed on the surface of mucous membranes. Incarcerated men performed acts of sodomy and violation, passed along terminal illness through their pustulent orifices. They lay with each other in sin. He would not go in. He would not permit it. His face was hot, flashes of pressure on his temples. His hands shook.

—An attorney!

—Soon guy, soon. Little busy right now.

—No please, whimpered Phillip as they unlocked the cage door. —No please no please no please . . . .

—Goddammit he's passing out there. Don't let him fall they'll charge our asses with brutality.

8:13

—How was it Ken? Dynamic tension there? You know what I say Ken, a handjob a day keeps the doctor away.

—The lady was Chinese or something.

—Asian I know Ken, the name of the place was a tipoff. Don't you like 'em Ken? No taste for the cultures of the Far East?

—They eat dogs.

—Well we all have our little habits Ken, now don't we. Next time it'll be All American Burger, buddy, 100% U.S. Grade A prime beef. Would you like that better?

—Anyway she didn't like me. She didn't do anything Decetes, she just rubbed my back.

—Wait Ken, hold it a minute. Are you telling me we didn't get our money's worth my boy?

—Nothing Decetes, she made me lie on my front the whole time.

—Ken you go sit in the car. I'll be back in a minute.

The receptionist looked wary when Decetes approached her. She had pink fingernails, long and curled.

—Leon B. Grossman. Young woman I wish to have a word with your supervisor.

—I am the supervisor.

—In that case I've got a bone to pick with you. My little friend out there did not get what I paid for.

—Just a moment. I'll discuss it with the girl.

She went through a door behind her. Decetes inspected her desk while she was absent. On a pad she had written *Wella Black Cherry 367 & Creme Developer.*

—Sorry, but Kim was afraid she'd throw up. She's just a trainee. Your friend's not something we see every day.

—I will be reimbursed, in that case.

—Nope. We have a strict policy. Time is money.

—Listen young woman, I work in the magazine industry. Believe me, you don't want a bad review.

—Your pathetic threat doesn't impress me, but I tell you what. I'm too tired for hassles. How about a quick five-minute freebie for yourself and we'll call it even.

—That will be satisfactory, said Decetes. —Not Kim though. I had her earlier today. Variety is the spice of life.

—All we have is Kims.

8:20

—I have to go home now, said Alice.

—Don't go, said the biker. —Please.

—I'm sorry, said Alice. —It's been a long day and all I wanted was a drink.

Walking back up to the beach she felt the night air sweep in behind her and blow her hair over her face. She recalled an instant of a dream, vague pink mountains in a desert that looked like the moon, and wished she could fly. A one-man wake for a bird. And yet that vendor, had her own eyes deceived her? He must be swimming, swimming underwater, dreaming of peace. Around him, swirling in the tide, ice-cream wrappers and spent balloons. A dream without anchors.

8:24

—Ginny! Jerry she's home!

—Leave me alone you make me sick, said Ginny, and mounted the stairs to her room.

—But Ginny we were worried!

—Stop right there young lady and apologize to your mother. You've put her through a lot. And where's the car?

—In the driveway, okay? I want some privacy for once or I'm leaving again and this time I won't come back.

—Don't talk that way to your mother.

—You didn't see what she did. You weren't there. She came right into class wearing her stupid housecoat and slippers. It was the worst thing that ever happened to me in my life so just shut up and leave me alone. I have to decide what to do.

—Ginny do not say shut up to your father.

—Riva just let her go. We'll talk about it later.

Ginny took the rest of the stairs three at a time. *Square root of 47962.15 = 219.00262, square root 14.798, square root 3.8469, square root 1.9613, square root 1.4.*

—Riva? There's a dwarf statuette in the outside garbage, Dopey or Grumpy or something, said her father. —And what the hell were you doing making a fool of yourself in public? You went to school in that piece-of-shit robe? No wonder she was goddamn traumatized.

8:30

—I made a healthy low-fat dinner since you're on a diet. Soup and salad. Why don't you just come sit down at the table and eat. I'm sure you're hungry after all the excitement.

—It says dildos all sizes $29.99.

—Give me that! If I have to lock my brother's file cabinet, I will.

—Can I have a glass of wine?

—I don't want to be responsible for one of your little seizures like the other night. I didn't want to mention it Barbara but my carpet had just been steam-cleaned. I don't know about you but I for one am not made of money. I have to count my pennies! A penny saved is a penny earned. Anyway I have a more suitable book you can read, called *The Book of Margery Kempe*. It's the spiritual diary of a woman who had seizures like yours, but she saw Jesus on many different occasions. I think you'll find it encouraging. It shows how special people are often God's dearest children. It's one of my own inspirational favorites.

—Huh.

—Phillip mentioned that you like to study the mind of Christ.

—The mind of Christ is shitty.

8:42

—That's settled Ken. I gave those Koreans the sharp side of my tongue. Never told you this Ken, but I fought in the Korean conflict. Speak the language fluently, like a native. Ho Chi Minh Ken. Those were the days Ken, we swooped down in our glorious silver machines Ken with white skin and blond hair and they thought we were gods. And we were Ken. Yes we were. Yours truly sowed his wild oats in the rice paddies Ken, drank American beer in the whorehouses Ken with pretty coffee-colored misses hanging off his arm.

—But don't I get to go back in?

—The death and the glory Ken, I saw them fall Ken. My brothers in arms. Choppers over the jungle Ken, yellow fever, malaria. Young boys dying in the marshes Ken, my brothers Ken, all my brothers. Their arms flung out Ken, their eyes open. Rain fell into their eyes Ken, rolled down their cheeks like tears. Rain fell heavy in the jungle Ken, the plants sweated and flowers burst forth, big flowers bright as fire. Once after the rain I thought I saw a flower Ken, a red flower on the wet frond of a fern. Went to pick it and wear it in my buttonhole but that was no flower Ken, that was the heart of a soldier. Those were the days Ken, death was our mother, our father and death was our child.

—So when do I get a handjob?

EVERYONE'S PRETTY

—Soon Ken soon. I gave those Kims the sharp side of my tongue Ken, you can lay money on that. Thankless my boy, the sacrifices we made and this is how they treat us now. The people of the world Ken, they have a short memory. I saw farmboys from Iowa give their lives for the Kims of this world, and now a lousy handjob is too much to ask. Ken, let us swing by the liquor store on our way home. Where's the car Ken?

—Gone.

—No time for joking Ken, we have an evening of strategy before us. We will use coins as armies Ken, and give them free range across a map of the world. The War Room Ken, where generals gather with Cuban cigars to plot the downfall of Castro. No Ken, no time for kidding right now. Where'd you repark the Pinto my son?

—It was gone when I got here. You said wait in the car but I got here and it was gone. See there's a Nissan in the space where it was, right there Decetes. Somebody musta lifted it.

8:53

—Ginny it's time for us to have a little talk, said her mother at the dinner table.

They were eating late because they hadn't eaten while they were waiting for her and then Ginny refused to come down right away and then her mother refused to eat if she wasn't at the table and her father came up and said *Can we please fucking eat* so she had to go down. Otherwise she'd get one of his serious talks that were even worse than her mother's because he thought he was being so hip and cool.

She concentrated on the salad, which was not as disgusting as the pot roast. Salad was normal, pot roast was not.

Gross with white fat. They cut it off a cow that had intestines and everything plus a brain and eyeballs, gross gross gross.

—I will not have you having relations and getting abortions just because the other girls do it.

—Just let her eat Riva, Christ, said her father. —No wonder she didn't want to come out of her room.

Ginny speared a leaf of iceberg lettuce, which was the safest food on her plate. She had to say it quick and get it over with. —I won't go back to school, she said crunching the lettuce. —But I'll go to that free program for geeks if you want.

—Ginny! gasped her mother and clasped her hands together. Her father left his mouth hanging open and his fork in midair.

9:03

Alice kicked off her shoes and opened the windows, shuffled junk mail, ALICE REEVE IS A $10,000,000 WINNER!, noticed the digital red 0 on her answering machine. Girls, parrots, vendors passed into the night. 000. Intangible. She would follow soon enough. One day floating near Jack the Sailor, unknowing as her molecules, now far away dispersed, were borne in waves toward the shores of Tahiti.

Her mother sat bereft in the hill country, watching TV. She sat there every night, unmoving. Alice used to be convinced that all she saw was colors dissolving and shapes that massed, separated and massed again.

Before she dialed she would have to have something to say. Something had to be known to be said, but she knew nothing save that she had nothing to say. Hated white walls. Hated her white curtains and white carpet. The phone rang.

—It's Ernie your favorite dancing queen. Come out with us. Jerome has a crush on you.

9:16

They sat on the curb, their feet in the gutter. Ken knew the workings of the camcorder now: pre-production was complete.

—Here Ken, take a swig of that. What can it harm Ken, no birds on this street. Firewater. I know what you're thinking Ken. You're thinking this is a man who almost gave his life for America, and now he's mounting a revolution. Is that what you were thinking Ken?

—I—

—This country, Ken, was great once. The land of the free Ken, the home of the brave. Therein lies the flaw Ken, the fatal flaw. Too free, Ken. Too brave.

—But—

—Yes Ken. Hoisted on its own petard. Free to buy Sony, Volkswagen and Mitsubishi Ken. Rape the land and poison the sea. Brave enough for Hiroshima Ken, and for Nagasaki.

—Gimme that.

A streetdweller, scabrous and stained, groped for Decetes's paper bag. His blond dreadlocks swung against Decetes's ear.

—Get outta here you bum. I'll fuck him up Decetes.

—Now Ken, no need for weapons. Ken, put the knife away. Yes my good man, please forage for your beverages elsewhere. That's a good man.

—See Decetes told you it would come in handy.

—Your first lesson Ken. The disenfranchised are our flock. Treat them kindly Ken, for they will be our corporals. Now Ken, I am treating you to an evening of the burlesque. It is a dying art Ken, but we will be present when it breathes its last.

Leon B. Grossman was a big spender, and generous to a fault.

9:24

Barbara was in Dean's room with her assigned reading. She had instructions to read ten pages of *The Book*. Only ten because her reading skills were probably not so hot. Then she could go to bed. Bucella had encouraged her to bring along the little dog Arf Arf: it was a Security blanket.

Phillip hadn't even called. No doubt he was out robbing savings bonds from Geriatrics. The note stuck to his fridge with a fruit magnet told him just what they thought of him. Bucella had written it herself, a rough draft first that was still in her purse.

"Dear" Phillip: Barbara is sick of your criminal habits (spying and Larceny) & in addition your Spousal Abuse. And Cruelty to Animals is also among your sins. Barbara likes pets and you have mistreated the Dog. Please Change your Ways, then she'll come Home.

At least she had her car back.

9:51

—Yeah man, said the antique black man. Phillip stood patiently in the corner, his hands clasped formally. They had placed him in a cell with a thin, spindly African-American grandfather in torn painter's overalls. He was, unfortunately, quite gregarious. —I was a singer man. I used to sing.

—I see, said Phillip.

—You know, all over the place, New Orleans, St. Louis, Chicago.

—I have never visited St. Louis myself, offered Phillip.

The man might be unstable, being a criminal and all. It was best to keep the conversation on an even keel. The eagles, unflappable, waited with their wings folded, weathering the storm.

—New Orleans there's a city for you. Sang and played the harmonica too, said the old man, and doubled over suddenly holding his stomach.

—Are you ill? inquired Phillip politely. He would not offer assistance. It could be a ploy: the man might be a pickpocket or a confidence artist. He had read about their sly tricks.

He waited, scrutinizing the top of the ancient head. It was bald and shone like polished wood. Phillip recalled a cherry table in his aunt's house, his aunt who had died of emphysema. When she was writing her will he had requested the table specifically, but she had left it to the Presbyterian church on the corner. So he had made the church a respectable offer for the table, which after all was pocked and scarred through many years of hard use, but they had sold it out from under him to a more foolhardy bidder.

His aunt had never even been a Presbyterian. She lived and died Episcopalian.

—No big deal man, said the old man. —It's one of them ulcers I think they said. He acts up time to time that little devil, I don't pay him no mind.

—A wise choice, said Phillip. —The body is an illusion. God works in the spirit.

—All right, crowed the little old man. —You said it.

10:07

—Dance with me, said Jerome.

—I prefer to drink, said Alice. —I'm better at it.

—You just like to watch, said Jerome.

10:14

—Here we are Ken, the promised land, said Decetes, tripping on the walkway. —Home from our epic voyage through the flesh. I am Odysseus!

—I gotta take a leak.

—The bushes are calling your name my boy. I see a lilac with the word *toiletbowl* written all over it.

Watching Ken amble toward the shrubbery, he realized he had a diplomatic rapprochement to perform. He had planned to stow Ken in the Pinto for the night, but the Pinto was AWOL. His cameraman must not be allowed to sneak away while he slept.

—Look lively Ken. Ken my man, didn't you wash that parrot off your arm? I think I see some crusty brain there Ken. Use the garden hose at the side of the house. My sister is a neatnik.

—Yeah I like your sister, she's got big bazooms, ventured Ken, shaking his tiny manfinger in the wind. Decetes could swear it was the size of a pinky. He stood clear.

—Ho Ken, slow down there Ken. My sister is not a sexual object. She is a female eunuch Ken.

—But—

—What can I tell you boy, sex and my sister just don't go together. She's trying to become a nun Ken, she reads up on the lives of saints and other hysterics. She saw a movie on

Bravo with some good-looking French virgin nuns in it Ken, and ever since then she's been trying to get Catholic. Wash yourself Ken, and wait outside while she and I discuss tonight's arrangements.

In the living room Bucella was arranging *House & Gardens* into symmetrical stacks.

—If I may say so Bucella, your face is suffused with an inner light. When I came in Bucella I mistook you for the Madonna.

—What do you want Dean.

—Just Christian charity Bucella.

—What.

—You remember the small man with the unfortunate facial mole? You were introduced this morning?

—Not formally. And if that's a mole the Taj Mahal is a condo.

—How cruel Bucella, you sound as bad as me. As the old me, Bucella. Not the new me. Because I'll tell you the truth Bucella, I went to a meeting. AA. That's where I met him.

She turned dumbfounded from the coffee table.

—You what?

—Yes Bucella. Alcoholics Anonymous. On Wilshire near Lincoln. Same time next week Bucella. Yes Bucella, it's a damn good group of people. They're fighters Bucella, and I respect them for that.

—Dean, my God. Are you lying?

—Bucella! I'm making of myself a new man. Acknowledging my Higher Power. I have accepted Jesus Christ as my personal savior. It came to me in a flash of blinding light Bucella. I thought I heard the archangel Gabriel singing to me from a bourbon on the rocks. "Dean Decetes," he said to me, "The road is clear before you. Throw down your soiled clothes Dean Decetes and join the ranks of the pure." He wanted to baptize me Bucella in the silver stream of faith, but I said I was unworthy. "I will try to be worthy," I said to the archangel Gabriel. "I will try." You may laugh Bucella, go ahead and laugh but this is the first day of the rest of my life.

She hedged closer and looked at him sharply.

—Dean, really? Really Dean?

—It's the right decision Bucella, I found the strength at last. Yes Bucella, I can face you and say it out loud: my name is Dean Decetes. I am an alcoholic.

—Really Dean?

—If you've never believed me before, believe me now Bucella.

—Dean—how do you feel?

—I feel good, I feel good. The scales are lifted from my eyes. But this guy, he's a tragic story Bucella. He served in the Vietnam conflict, covert actions. Small size was an asset to the Army, he could wiggle through foxholes and the like, but afterward they abandoned him. When the war was over he came home and lived on the streets. Led to liquor, drugs Bucella, his childhood sweetheart rejected him. A circus midget she was Bucella, from Tallahassee.

—You better not be making this up Dean.

—Making it up? A man's life we're talking about here. I would never lie about war Bucella. War's no joke to me.

—It was a joke at the time Dean, if I recall you were incarcerated for dodging the draft.

—My youth Bucella, Canada is a beautiful country. But this guy Bucella, he's tried everything to get better, tries to get work but people discriminate Bucella. An ugly dwarf does not have it easy in America. He's my sponsor Bucella, been in AA ten years, and let me tell you he's a good Christian Bucella, family's Catholic, he loves Jesus and the Virgin, you can ask him yourself. All I'm requesting, I'm begging a little hospitality for this man Bucella, a bed for the night.

—Dean if he has such a loving family why doesn't he have somewhere to sleep?

—Lives in Orange County now. Comes in once a week for the meetings, been with this same AA chapter for years. He usually goes home but I kept him here talking, shooting the breeze Bucella, about Jesus Christ, and now he's a little tired.

—Just this once okay Dean? He gives me the creeps. When he was in here before all he did was stare at my endowments.

—I spoke to him about that Bucella, not his fault. It's an eye-level problem. You have a heart of gold Bucella. He'll be grateful.

Outside, around at the side of the house, Ken was drinking from the hose, slurping at the stream like a mutt.

—You're in AA with me all right Ken? You're a Christian, you were in the Army in Vietnam and did covert actions, okay Ken?

—Army?

—Yes Ken. Remember to say you love the Virgin Mary, family's Catholic okay Ken?

—Family?

—Just play along Ken. You clean? Come on in.

Ken shuffled in behind him, wiping his mouth on his sleeve.

—I love a virgin, said Ken to Bucella.

—*The* Virgin, right Ken? He's aphasic Bucella.

—I sure love a Catholic virgin in the family, said Ken, nodding.

—Pardon me?

—The aphasia, you know like George Bush Senior Bucella? A side effect of Agent Orange. It's the military-industrial complex Bucella, see what it can do to a good honest citizen?

10:38

There was a telephone in an alcove next to the men's bathroom. Alice's ears were ringing but she knew what she had to do. She grappled with her wallet and finally extracted the card. Distracted momentarily by its rude silver sheen, in which her eyes shone soft and large and her nose was a snout, she read the blurred directions on the back and typed some digits into the keypad.

—U.S. Sprint how can I help you?

—I have to call my mother, said Alice.

10:53

Ken was safely ensconced in an afghan on the living room couch, sleeping like a baby, and Bucella was washing pots in the kitchen. Decetes would have to strategize alone, in his boudoir. First, however, he would fortify himself in the backyard, one man alone with his sustenance, the crystal liquid sparkling under moonlight, surrounded by bounteous nature in the form of geraniums, tiger lilies and Spanish moss.

Possibly he could catch a glimpse of the teenage strumpet, disrobing before bed. The yellow rectangle of her window was often a beacon in the wilderness.

He quietly removed his spare fifth from its hiding place behind Bucella's ancient *World Book Encyclopedia* set and tiptoed out the front door.

Unfortunately, the window of grace was unlit. Decetes stationed himself in a butterfly chair and toasted the Big Dipper.

The parrot, the poor parrot. A perky chap with a twinkle in his beady eye. Damn their eyes! Decetes had always had a fondness for birds. In the new kingdom, that poor martyred creature would perch on his wrist, its wings and beak tinged with gold.

—Nice night! How's it going man, said the businessman from next door, stepping out his sliding back door and lifting his glass.

—Things are looking up buddy, said Decetes across the hedge.

—Glad to hear it, said the businessman, and belched. — My wife's back, my daughter's back, we're one big happy fucking family.

—American dream, said Decetes, and took a generous swig. He had come to the woods to live deliberately, but the Rolex-sporting Cro Magnon was disturbing his peace.

Still, there might be Chivas Regal in it for him.

—Tell me something man, said the suit. —What do you think of my wife?

—Ho there, said Decetes, and raised a deferential palm to signify abstention. His daily quota for beatings had already been exceeded. —I make it a point of honor never to think about other men's wives.

—No seriously, said the suit, and tipped back his tumbler. —I mean would you say she's looking good for her age? Just between you and me, I feel like she's let herself go.

—I myself, mused Decetes, —am a firm believer in extra-marital intercourse. I was married once, and faithful as the day is long. Sure I was tempted. Administrative assistants and Ivy League account managers with blond hair and big hooters throwing themselves in my face over sushi and saké, you know how it is, but I restrained myself. Then she left me for a petrochemical mogul. Since then it's every man for himself. Fidelity, my friend, is for pets and mutual funds.

—Ha ha, said the suit. —Administrative assistants, ha.

—Alice honey are you coming to the service?

—I no, no I can't, see it would be—

—Please Alice honey—

A dark graceful hand touched hers on the receiver and climbed up her arm. The chest against her back was muscled and smooth.

—Jerome's here.

—Because Alice he really loved you sweetie he just didn't know how to show it.

—See that's where you're wrong mother he showed it, he really did, she said.

—Alice honey we have to forgive and forget!

Her skirt was sliding up over her hips and there were lips on her neck. She closed her eyes and was dizzy.

—Sorry mother but I can't do that, she said. —I've been trying to forget all my life but forgiving is out of the question.

—But Alice forgiveness is—

She covered the receiver and turned in the circle of the arms, but her legs were weak and he was holding her up. — Isn't Ernie going to be upset?

—Ernie knows, he's not the jealous kind.

—Lord giveth sweetiepie—

—Relax, whispered Jerome.

Jerome was soft and hard. Her feet came off the floor and she closed her eyes. The quick faces of passersby were moons in the shadows, almost invisible. She was drifting without landmarks, drunk enough to feel airborne but not motion sickness. She remembered carnivals, the pier. You entrusted yourself to the arc of a ferris wheel, the swing of old machinery in cool air, with organ-grinding music far away on the ground. The wall was gritty and warm, years of hands, arms, clothing rubbing into her skin. Leavings of strangers, invisible remnants. Somewhere a sea of them, joined by the coincidence of space. She stretched one arm out along the surface, spreading her fingers. The receiver bobbed softly on her shoulder.

—If you could be here and sit in the pew with me Alice—

—I can't, she sighed.

—But honey I'm all alone, came from years distant like a low wind through the grass, and Alice thought she felt the wall curve behind her.

11:32

—My name is Dean and I'm an alcoholic, he practiced as he staggered toward bed. All the lights were out. Blundering his way through the dark, He stubbed his toe on the door to his room and swore in a whisper.

Inside, he discarded clothing onto the floor. Light must be forfeited: Bucella had eyes in the back of her head. She saw through wallboard and plaster and picked out drunkenness in the infrared scopes of her cornea like a sniper on the grassy knoll.

He felt his way to the sofabed. Wide arms came up to clasp his own and pull him down. She was as loamy as the earth, as warm and thick as mud. She was a barrel, a cauldron of flesh.

—You came back! he said. —Earth mother. Angel! Messenger of my glory.

Forthwith he blessed the angel with his staff.

Chapter the Eighth

Hymns are sung; a coup d'état is attempted;
and a mummy is found in Beverly Hills

—You may rest assured, said Phillip smartly in taking leave of his erstwhile jailer, —I am planning to enlist the services of an attorney. Your apologies come far too late. The treatment I have received is indefensible. An outrage! And a violation of this nation's Constitution.

   —Go man go, chortled his cellmate, waving and doubling over in pain.

8:56

They were throwing rocks at her Beloved. Thin children on the bare hill ran at the back of the crowd, and Bucella at the front, but she was pressing against the throng, throwing herself at their mercy in a frenzy of Begging. —Don't hurt him!

she cried, her cheeks stained with tears. —Don't you know who he is? But they were strong and mean-faced and threw her aside and trampled her underfoot. Ahead stood Ernest in white rags, his legs torn, in a field of thistles. His arms were thrown Wide, his face was to the Heavens. —Why hast thou forsaken me?

She lay on the ground where she fell, in a heap with the sand washing over her, blowing across the dunes. It covered her legs and her stomach until the rain began to fall. Warm rain, heavy drops, and then she saw one of the stone-throwers standing over her, smiling. An ugly man, a small ugly man. Behind him not thunderclouds but the ceiling, writhing with plaster Worms. Beneath it, her open bedroom door.

—My God! and she sat up shrieking, pulling the covers over herself. The warm rain on her stomach stuck the sheet against her skin, and the Midget zipped up his Fly and scurried out.

9:04

Alice woke, temples throbbing, facing a pale lavender wall striped white where the sun glanced over the curved backs of slats. She was on a wide sofa with a flannel sheet spread over the peaks of her knees and tucked under her chin. Her neck and shoulders were sore, but it was a mild ache. It was almost soothing. She stayed immobile in the calm, gazing ahead. In an oval mirror she could see the ceiling reflected, a pool of light. Then there was the ticking of claws over hardwood, a rush of weight, and the milky opaque eyes of a dog.

His paws laid on her chest, he stretched his body over her and panted in her face. She stared at the eyes. Blue-white. No pupils only irises.

—Down boy, said Ernie.

Alice looked up: he was standing at the living-room door in a brown silk dressing gown. The dog laid his chin on his paws and blinked.

—Disobedient cur. Feeling better darling?

—I could feel worse, said Alice. —A headache. Should I be apologizing for something?

—No apologies. Everything's fine. Tea or coffee? Let me get you some pills and a glass of water first. You're dehydrated. Down boy.

—What happened to his eyes?

—Who knows, he was a stray. He was blind when I found him. You stay right there.

The dog lay warm and heavy on her.

—Here you go, said Ernie, bustling back in, tipping two round pills onto her palm. —Sleep in, come into the office after lunch. Take the other half of your sick day. I'll slice a grapefruit for you before I go, espresso's in the pot, and the door locks when you close it. There are extra toothbrushes in the vanity. Brand new never used. I said *down*.

The dog raised itself lazily and slumped to the floor beside her.

—Sugar bowl's on the silver tray on the counter.

—Ernie didn't I—?

—Wouldn't anyone Alice? Don't worry he's safe. Actually he's even prudish. Usually. Wait, I have some new shoes to show you.

She trailed a hand over the dog's long back and stared at the plants on the sill till he came back.

—I grew the rosemary from seed. Here, do you like them?

He swiveled an ankle right and left, from the toe.

—I like them.

—Kenneth Cole for women. Twelve wide.

—Beautiful. But are you sure—

—Alice dear, I live vicariously always. I really should change and get going. Make sure you finish that grapefruit. You don't eat enough. There's a sesame loaf in the breadbox and honey in the cabinet. Toast wouldn't do you any harm either.

He rounded the corner and she was alone again. The blind dog sighed and closed his eyes. Warm light, considering it was morning.

9:08

That was it, the last straw. Dean brought perverts and degenerates into her home, but it would never happen again. Bucella tightened the sash of her robe around her waist and took the stairs three at a time. The Midget was nowhere to be seen. He was hiding in the microwave, maybe. She checked the kitchen and the living room and then pushed open Dean's door without knocking. The room was dark and smelled putrid. Then she saw them and slammed the door rapidly.

She stood there facing the closed door. Breathe in, breathe out. But finally she had to open it again.

Dean was curled like a fetus in the embrace of Barbara, who lay naked on her back, splay-legged, on the soiled Couch of his Infamy.

Bucella picked up her hardcover Concordance and threw it at his face. It only hit him on the shoulder. He raised his head groggily. Barbara stirred and groaned.

—Get up and get out, said Bucella through gritted teeth. —You disgust me. I have never seen anything worse than this. You have sunk as low as you can this time, Dean. I feel like throwing up. She is mentally challenged. And married!

—Earth mother, mumbled Dean.

—Did you even ask her if she wanted to? This woman has been abused, Dean. She is vulnerable. You are the lowest of the low.

—But she—

—Shut up and put your clothes on and get out. For good. I really mean it this time Dean.

Barbara opened her eyes.

—Now Dean. I mean now. Or I call the police.

—Bucella you are overreacting, he grumbled, yawning and rooting in his windward ear with a finger. His rude Sausage was shamelessly exposed. —Do I have to remind you Jesus Christ is my personal savior?

—Wild wayout kinky.

—Please Barbara, cover yourself. I am embarrassed. Dean, I'm not standing for any more. I want you out in fifteen minutes flat. And take all your things. Get off her now!

He hoisted himself off, Barbara jiggling inertly as he stepped over her onto the floor and stood scratching his armpits.

—Now get dressed and go. Take the midget with you. And don't touch her again. You have fifteen minutes.

9:23

There was a rooster in the henhouse. His beak was nobly arched, his claws sharp, his feathers preened: but the old hen was squawking again, flustered by his virile displays. She pecked like a hen and spat like a camel.

Food, water, clothing, shelter. Decetes was not a man to overlook the practical necessities. He pulled on two balled dirty socks of old gray argyle and made for the closet where camping gear was stowed. Ah yes. A one-man tent in excellent condition, a sleeping bag, pegs and a groundsheet. He bundled them up under his arms and snuck them out the back door to deposit them with stealth, always vigilant in his senses as was any beast of prey, behind the trees at the far reaches of Bucella's backyard. She would not think to look for him there; he could sleep soundly at night, until she relented finally, as she always did. He stashed his bundle behind a bougainvillea.

Then back inside again, to forage what he could, to salvage and retreat, with haste, with cunning, and with guile.

9:30

It began and ended in calumny. She was a strumpet, a many-headed beast. He that toucheth pitch shall be defiled therewith. The handwriting was the same!

She had invaded his home, kidnapped his wife and left a second note for him, of threat and accusation. And on the door a random insult. It must have taken place during his incarceration, retaliation for the episode in the saloon. Evidently there were two Alices: the vicious slut and the hiding virgin. He must not forget who had cried out to him in the wilderness. But wait. Even psychiatrists, in their false medicine that abnegated the mind of Christ, had a name for it. A secular label for a battle of the spirit: multiple personality disorder. Within her Satan warred with the virgin brides, and took disparate forms. He must cleave to those virgin angels, blond heads bowed and demure, salty peaches hidden to every man but him. Their need was coming to a crisis.

And Barbara, that traitor to his mastery. That rotten vessel. He raised his head and looked up at the plaque on the wall. *Spirit is the real and the eternal; matter is the unreal and tem-*

poral. He was beginning to see. Spirit was his and raw matter theirs. The vital opposition was not what he had assumed it to be. In his humility he had believed the weakness lay in himself. He had been wrong, he had permitted his natural pity to draw a veil of ignorance over his eyes. It was, in fact, not the case that every man's spirit must act within him to quench the baser impulses of meat: rather a man such as he embodied spirit. The task of spirit was to rule over flesh. Rule, vanquish, extirpate. He would bring them both to heel.

He washed himself with antibacterial soap. Dear Phillip! *Get thee behind me, Satan.* Matthew 16:23. Rinsed and washed again. *The dogs shall eat Jezebel.* Kings 21:23. Rinsed. Washed again. Rinsed. Exodus 15:7. *Thou sentest forth thy wrath.*

9:38

Decetes hurled a clod of earth at the window of grace, and when it provoked no response lobbed a handful of gravel from the drive. Finally the girl next door showed her face at the glass.

—Need a little favor, said Decetes when she grudgingly raised the frame. She wore a pink T-shirt that read HELLO STUPID.

—Are you crazy? she asked sleepily, and pushed a wisp from her forehead. —Why would I do you a favor?

—I know that, in the past, I have employed dubious methods in our friendly negotiations, and I regret it. A man has needs. However, if you do this one thing for me I give you my solemn oath: I will never blackmail you again.

—Yeah right, she drawled, and yawned.

—Please, said Decetes. —I am a man of my word. No more blackmail.

—I'm getting out of here in three weeks. So I don't care what you do.

—I am sorry to hear that, said Decetes. Indeed it was distressing news. From here on in he would pay for his floorshows. Leon B. Grossman had splurged on lap dances, and his credit was shot. —But do this for me out of the goodness of your heart. I have always relied on the kindness of strangers.

She cocked her head to one side dreamily.

—Tell me what it is and I'll think it over.

—I need two bottles of whiskey from your father's liquor cabinet.

She disappeared inside and returned with a purple hairbrush, which she plied dreamily. Decetes was becoming impatient. It had been almost five hours since his last drink.

—Okay, she said. —If you do something for me.

—Name your price.

—Take all your clothes off slowly and sing a song while you're doing it.

—Surely you jest.

—Nope. No strip, no booze. I was going to make you bark like a dog, but that's too easy.

—You drive a hard bargain. What assurance do I have that you'll give me the goods?

—I'm a woman of my word.

—I need a taste before we begin. Slip me a shot out the back door.

—Nope. You gotta do it stone-cold sober.

—My dear child, I am never stone-cold sober.

—I don't have all day and neither do you. They'll be up soon. And sing quietly or they'll wake up for sure.

—Fuck. Okay, said Decetes. Humiliation was merely a means to an end. As such it was grossly underrated. —Here goes.

9:49

—Say it with me Barbara, said Bucella. Barbara sat at the kitchen table eating a banana. —It'll make you feel better. Almighty God, unto whom all hearts are open.

— . . . Mighty God onto him. . . .

—All desires known, and from whom no secrets are hid.

— . . . All desires none, and from him secrets are hid. Can I get another banana?

—It was my fault too Barbara! I forgot to make Dean sleep in another room. Cleanse the thoughts of our hearts by the inspiration of thy Holy Spirit.

—Clean the thoughts by instigation of the . . . roly Spit . . . .

—That we may perfectly love thee and worthily magnify thy holy Name.

She took the peel out of Barbara's hand and placed it in the compost. Barbara reached out over the table and broke another banana off the bunch.

—We do earnestly repent, and are heartily sorry for these our misdoings; the remembrance of them is grievous unto us; the burden of them is intolerable. Amen.

9:51

—Bring me my bow of burning gold, warbled the old pervert, hopping while he pulled off a shoe. —Bring me my arrows of desire. Bring me my spear, oh clouds unfold, he grunted as the second shoe fell onto the driveway. —Bring me my char-i-ot of fire!

—You have to dance.

—I will not cease . . . from mental fight, he sang, fumbling with his shirt buttons and wiggling his hips. —Nor shall my sword sleep in my hand.

—What kind of song is that, she said.

He had a saggy chest and a hairy stomach.

—Till we have built Jerusalem, and he pulled down his pants. He was wearing orange boxer shorts. The waistband was loose and they fell to his ankles. —On England's green and pleasant land.

Mondo pathetic. That was a good line though, about the kindness from strangers. She was going to use that for sure.

—Satisfied? he asked.

—Obviously more than your girlfriend. Oh yeah I forgot. You don't have a girlfriend.

She crept out of her room in bare feet. Her parents' room door was still closed. In the basement she found a bourbon and a scotch. The lech was tying his shoes on the patio.

—Those are half-empty!

—Yeah but more than these he'll miss 'em.

—Ginny? What are you doing down there?

Her mother, screeching from upstairs.

—That's it they're up, she whispered, and shoved the bottles into his hands.

—Thank you, said the pervert, —every woman is the gift of a world.

She had just closed the doors when her mother came down.

—Ginny did I hear something?

—You always hear something. The distributive law for series follows from the fact that the sum of an infinite series is determined by its nth partial sum, which is finite.

—Won't you eat a wholesome breakfast this morning honey?

—Only if you do a favor for me.

—What's that sweetiepie?

—Graph a simple polynomial.

10:08

Even in the folds where the drapes fell there was restfulness. The order of Ernie's chairs, sofa, table was an order of stopped time, a monument to care. He seldom drank, but kept the bar stocked; didn't smoke, but ashtrays were discreetly placed. She sat on a chair, sipping from her cup and staring at a small painting of a saint, pierced by arrows, face illuminated. Her own face was not illuminated. In the silence she raised her cup again.

—I don't want to go home, she said aloud.

The dog heaved itself up from beside the sofa and trotted over to her feet, where it collapsed again and began to snore.

Her coffee was cooling, and hating Ray had been the rope of her life. Now Ray, waned away on the jaws of a tumor, was only the memory of her skin, of her arms, shoulders, atoms. Ray was in molecules. He would never be nothing. He was inside and outside, everywhere. Once you were who you were there you were: it was impossible to know who she would have been without Ray. She wouldn't have been without Ray. That was biology. And then there were the social sciences.

Hate had been all she had. She used to think it was splendid, would outlive her, a mote spinning in space, unseen. But now it was hope she dreamed of, spinning there endlessly. Hatred was boring.

She looked at a vase, a plain silver vase filled with yellow tulips, on an end table. She put her coffee cup down, got up and walked over to it, idly slid the tulips out by their cool slick stems. Looked at the vase. It was cold and lovely. She put the tulips back. There had been something wrong with the rope of her hate, a weakness in its fibers, it was frayed from beginning to end and slipped and slipped forever. What was wrong with it? Not what people said: not its impulses. Loyalty had to be conditional, otherwise it was only submission. The impulses were not wrong. But something was. She moved a tulip for symmetry, then another. That was it. Hate was the arrangement of flowers in a hollow place.

It was not resistance. Only resistance was splendid.

Prozac said the shrink once, but Alice said she didn't want to be a permutation of chemicals. If that was all that was all. Chicken Little the sky is falling: hand me my umbrella. But then she went to booze instead, a golden parachute.

And she let herself fall, since falling she forgot who she was, and so even forgot Ray woven through her bones and her cells. Without herself she could be with the others: any and all. Hell was in the molecules first.

—Where's the good life? she asked the dog. He blinked.

But *this* was the good life. This.

10:19

Decetes struck out down the road with his whiskey and the camcorder stashed in Bucella's Girl Guide backpack. Ken was idling at the corner, hands in his pockets, kicking at dirt.

—Today, Ken, announced Decetes gravely, —we make the movie of my life. It will convert the needy millions. They have no leader Ken, and no future. But soon they will have both.

—My gut hurts.

—Ah yes I forgot Ken, you are not an airy plant like me. Not a creature of spirit, feeding on the ether, the winds and the stars, but an honest, sturdy beast of the earth. We can make a pit stop before the triumph begins Ken. We have all the time in the world. What'll it be? IHOP or Denny's?

10:36

Her air freshener swung from the rearview mirror like a pendulum. Pine Scent this way, Pine Scent that. It was the hour to right wrongs.

The air freshener made a rhythm as she drove, saying yes, yes, yes. Zamphir flute. A phoenix rose from the ashes, and it was her! In her floral silk blouse that had to be dry-cleaned and therefore could only be worn on special Occasions.

The castles of Debauchery were crumbling in her wake: for she had finally cleaned House. She could set forth with a clear conscience and would not be like Lot's wife turning to a pillar of salt, for Gomorrah Ancient City of Palestine was behind her now, and it would stay that way. Before when Dean had begged to her she had always thought of him when he was little and crying for their sick mother. And she had thought of Dean when their mother died, standing in the kitchen in his funeral suit, barely as tall as the table, and of their father drunk and sleeping through the time for the funeral and how because of him they never went. And Dean stood in the kitchen in his funeral suit waiting till it grew dark outside.

But she had to face the facts. That little boy was gone now.

Anyway you could not think of dry-cleaning or Dean when choirs of archangels were singing. You could not think of it when the sun was rising on a new Dawn. As soon as she got to work she would steal back the letter from Phillip's desk and slip it under Ernest's door. Glory glory!

The gas gauge read E. She pulled into a gas station. With the nozzle in the fuel hatch she closed her eyes. The gas pulsed through. Dean deflowered the Innocent. Barbara was annoying but being Challenged she was also a babe in the woods. Jesus wept.

Bucella was feeling nervous, or maybe it was Acid Indigestion. When Joan of Arc stood in front of her solemn Judges she was probably nervous too, since they didn't have Due Process Under the Law back then. But she had remained unflinching. Joan did not worry about dry-cleaning, rather she raised her head proudly to her Tormentors. Even when the flames were licking at her knees.

Regular Self. Premium Self.

On the wall beside the gas station lot a kid was spray-painting graffiti. I FUCKED YER SIS.

The pump clicked.

—You stop that! yelled Bucella, releasing the handle.

The kid turned around. He wore a baseball cap backwards on his head. He scowled and turned back to his work. T, E.

—You stop that obscenity now or I'll call the police!

—Shut your face, said the boy. R. —Already done anyways.

Behind the wall were tall trees and a clock in a tower.

—Whadda you care? Not your wall.

—It's everyone's wall, said Bucella. —That's obscene!

—Yeah well I'm everyone too so fuck you lady.

And he sauntered off, capping his spray can.

11:01

Decetes had given Ken a back issue to read as they made their way to HQ. He insisted on reading it as they walked. Unfortunate, mused Decetes, that Ken had not come with a halter and lead. He was meandering in the direction of a mailbox, his nose in the centerfold. His sneakers had mouths at the front and flapped as he stepped. Still, far be it from Decetes to intercede.

—Unhh!

—Whoops-a-daisy Ken, remember this simple rule. Every action has an equal and opposite reaction. Sir Isaac Newton, a colleague of mine. Stick with me boy, I'll show you the ropes.

—But Decetes, this gal's got a ding-dong.

—First, Ken, those are the advertisements. The fact that we print them does not constitute an endorsement. Second, you render a disservice when you refer to the male member as a "ding-dong." Have some pride, Ken. What you call a ding-dong, Ken, is the first wonder of the world. Forget the hanging gardens of Babylon Ken, forget the statue of Zeus and the temple at Ephesus. Nary a one compares to the ding-dong. Without semen Ken where would we be today? There is much that you owe to your organ Ken. The will to live, for example.

11:04

Exiting the building Phillip passed his neighbor returning to his own apartment, wearing frayed bedroom slippers over bare feet. He executed a curt nod with his customary sangfroid. The man was untrustworthy. He was frequently unshaven and operated a coin laundromat at the corner in which transients were often to be seen, lounging on formica tables designed, purchased and designated by the management for the folding of clothes. Before the acquisition of the Kenmore washing machine/drier combination from Sears, at significant personal expense, Phillip had made use of the facilities there on no fewer than three separate occasions. He had developed the practice of taking his own Lysol, with which he sprayed the tables before folding his garments upon them. On his third visit, the table he preferred to use was, at the moment his drying cycle was complete, occupied by a sleeping transient. Phillip had woken him and asked him to remove his person therefrom, at first politely, then with increasing steadfastness of purpose.

The transient had refused adamantly, claiming other tables were free. But the free tables were also inferior tables. Phillip was compelled to spray the table, therefore, with the transient still on it. The transient's eyes began to water from the Lysol but he refused to budge; Phillip continued to spray until his can was empty; the transient, sobbing but stubborn, ingested Lysol in some volume and subsequently coughed up blood. Blood was a notorious health liability. Phillip had been forced to return to his home with his laundry unfolded. The resultant wrinkles had forced him to iron.

Reaching the curb where his rental was parked, his eye lit upon a pile of trash awaiting the truck. All was not right. He stepped closer cautiously. Atop a clear trash bag there was a rodent. It was small, yellow in color, and dead. From its mouth a tongue protruded. On its behind was a massive growth.

Phillip stepped back quickly and extracted a Kleenex from his pocket pack, which he swiftly placed over his mouth and nose.

He must put two and two together. His neighbor had been wearing bedroom slippers, and no outdoor apparel. There could only be one agent of this atrocity, for the rodent sat atop the trash, not beneath it. The rodent was a recent deposit. Phillip turned and walked briskly back up the stairs. He tapped firmly on his neighbor's door.

—Yeah?

The man was smoking a cigarette. His terrycloth robe was open to expose a filthy red undershirt.

—Mr. Grossman, are you the responsible party?

—Responsible for what?

—The rodent, Mr. Grossman. What else?

—Yeah, my daughter's hamster. She's at UCLA, moved to Westwood. Thing died. Good riddance is what I say. I woulda flushed it but it was too big.

—You can't do that. There are laws against it. The creature is diseased. It has a bubo. You must remove it immediately.

—Get outta here, it's a dead hamster that's all.

—Animal control must be notified. They will remove it. I would also advise contacting the Centers for Disease Control and Prevention. They are trained professionals. If you do not remove it at once I will call them myself.

—Go ahead and call. I don't give a shit.

—War, famine, pestilence and plague. My Lord!

—Leon what is this?

—Don't worry I got it taken care of. Guy's some kind of lunatic. Listen mister you're paranoid. It's a fucking dead hamster. Big deal.

—I will contact Animal Control. You will be prosecuted to the fullest extent of the law.

—Get outta my face.

The door was slammed.

11:35

There was a different security guard on duty in the lobby, ignorant, luckily, of Decetes's exile from paradise. He lifted nary a finger against them, and Ken, following with the camcorder held up to his face, encountered only a door edge to hinder his passage.

Also, Alan H.'s office was unlocked. It was a peaceful coup without bloodshed, a swift and stealthy ambush. Much had been learned, in terms of military strategy, from the Indians.

Decetes established himself behind the desk in Alan H.'s armchair in a lordly fashion. After taping him seating himself with dignity, Ken put down the camcorder and busied himself with a life-sized inflatable doll. She was a deluxe model: 3D eyelashes, spongy breasts and a plug-in vibrating unit. Alan H. had a room full of free loot from mail-order adult entertainment merchandisers. The spoils of war were bounteous.

—Tape this, said Decetes.

Ken dropped his doll reluctantly and lifted the camcorder again. Decetes swiveled in his chair and positioned himself in front of a full-color poster of a large-breasted model. It was a magazine cover from two years ago.

—I am Dean Decetes. I am the instrument of the masses, and this magazine will henceforth be their voice.

11:47

—Alice they found a man dead in a Dumpster this morning in Beverly Hills of all places, it was on the radio. Mummified darling, can you believe it? When I go I wouldn't mind being mummified. Nefertiti or maybe Isis. Is there a mummification service you can get? I mean they have cryogenics.

—But they scoop out your entrails Ernie. They put them in jars.

—Ooh I wouldn't like that.

—Embalmers do it too. Not the jars. But the scooping.

—Death is so tacky. But listen hon I need a little favor. I forgot my nylons and I'm going straight to Jerome's after work. Do you think you could bring them when you come in?

—Just tell me where they are.

—In the closet there's a chest of drawers. Top drawer. They're still in the package. Navy blue with white diamonds, my Kelly Girl Special. Have to go sweetie, my other line.

The walk-in closet was dedicated to Lola: long spangled dresses, fake-fur stoles, new Christian Dior costume earrings on plastic backings, wigs on styrofoam heads, corsets, eyeliner, eyelash curlers and lipstick. Brassieres in white mesh baskets. There was gold lamé and chenille, silk skirts and satin blouses. In the top drawer of the chest she found packages of nylons neatly stacked. Control-Top X-Large.

In a cluster of lavender potpourri hearts and yellowed silk flowers was an enamel box. She opened it and the porcelain ballerina began to turn on her dais: Brahms's lullaby. There were no words, but Alice heard them with the notes, a ghost behind the melody. Rock-a-bye baby, in the treetops.

Alice sat down on the floor in a pile of silky gloves and twisted scarves and waited to cry.

CHAPTER THE NINTH

A Rubber Ducky saves the day; the Black Plague is
narrowly averted; a Conquest goes awry; and the
Prince loses a loyal footsoldier

In *Sleeping Beauty* everyone in the castle fell asleep for a century. The castle was overgrown with vines, the dogs were sleeping on the hearth, old men slept on their chairs with white beards growing out along the floor and children breathed deeply, with closed eyes, beside their dusty fallen toys. No one grew old, they just slept. All so that once upon a time the Prince could hack with his sword through the thorns and morning glories that covered the walls and find the Princess young and golden-haired and beautiful, asleep in a position that certainly emphasized her good looks, for example not drooling on the pillow or snoring.

In *Sleeping Beauty* they never thought of the fact that all the servants and probably everyone else except the Princess had obligations and relatives outside the castle, and when they woke up after one hundred years all their friends and families would be dead. So it was only a Happy Ending for Sleeping Beauty and the Prince. For everyone else it was a nightmare. A lot of them probably had payments to make on their cottages or whatever, their mortgages were probably foreclosed by the bank while they were sleeping. Their pets all died of starvation, their kids were orphaned and became Problem Adolescents, and neighbors ransacked their houses for the silverware.

But she Bucella could not be Sleeping Beauty because she did not have a castle, just her bungalow in Culver City that was rented. Instead of a castle, scenic mountains or a Sunrise all she had to look at while she waited for Ernest to come and sweep her up was Chichén Itzá Historic Site of Ancient Mayan Temple, the grainy plastic arms of her swivel chair, the vertical files and the c-prompt on her screen. Plus Garfield the fat stupid cat.

Okay she was throwing that out. It was old. She ripped it off the bulletin board and stuffed it in her trashcan.

Now all there was on the board was Chichén Itzá Historic Site of Ancient Mayan Temple, Employee Dress Code, and her favorite quotation from *Revelations of Divine Love*. *It behoved that there should be sin; but all shall be well, and all shall be well, and all manner of thing shall be well.* If Joan of Arc worked here she would be fired for not adhering to the Employee Dress Code.

The fluorescent tubes on the ceiling were giving her a migraine. Who could be noble with fluorescent tubes? It was the wrong Atmosphere. The history of Now was not heroic because it had no Atmosphere. Dean didn't know anything about history. All he knew about was Fornication, although he was fond of using many big words that he apparently learned at the University of Southern California before he was kicked out for a number of egregious Honor Code violations, *including cheating, plagiarism, and the commission of criminal misdemeanors* as it said in the letter, which she still remembered because she had to open it herself. By that time she was the Legal Guardian, being older.

She looked at her hand on the mouse pad and it was shaking. What if he came in now, right this minute? Glory glory when she wasn't even ready? Check in the mirror. She swivelled her chair and there he Was! Lordy Lord. He stood there with his hands clasped, bowed over and humble like always. So modest. Glory!

—I'm sorry to bother you Bucella. I was just hoping you might be able to help me.

—Oh! Yes . . .

—It's a personal matter Bucella, and I could use some good advice.

He sat down on her guest chair and placed his hands on his knees. Palpitations. Heart murmurs ran in her family. She had to act calm and serene. She picked up her desk calendar. *Columbus Day October 14.*

—Let me tell you what happened. When I got into my office this morning, there was an envelope under the door—

—Yes!—

—which contained a letter. It seemed to be from an anonymous admirer, and I was deeply touched—

—Oh!—

—I was certainly . . . moved . . . but what I need your help with, Bucella, is—

—You—

—See I have to find a way—and maybe you can help me with this—to let the person know that I was deeply touched, but I can't engage in a—how should I put this—an intimate relationship with her. Of a physical nature.

—Oh . . .

—It's impossible for me, and it will always be impossible. I'm sure you know what I'm talking about, but I don't want to trouble you Bucella.

—No . . .

—So I was wondering if you could keep an ear to the ground, and if you find out anything, you know, about my anonymous friend, maybe you could let me know, so that I could contact her. And explain. Because obviously I can't go around asking staff if they've sent me anonymous letters. But I know you're on good terms with everyone. I wouldn't want to upset whoever it is; it's just that I—you understand—I don't have those kinds of relationships anymore.

—No of course . . .

—Physical relationships. With members of the fairer sex. I know you understand, Bucella, and I can rely on your discretion.

—Yes . . .

—Thank you Bucella. I appreciate it. I'm so sorry for the interruption. But it means so much to have your help.

After he retired she sat staring at the space where he had sat. Then she swivelled her chair and reached up and unpinned *Chichén Itzá Historic Site of Ancient Mayan Temple* and looked at it.

It was Resplendent Nature.

12:19

—Ken please control yourself. Put her down, there is business at hand. And a word of advice my boy, it will chafe unless you use a lubricant.

—Vat are you doink here?

In the doorway was the German nationalist from Personnel, the Wagnerian rhino. She had her square hands on her hips.

—Answer me plees. You are not authorized.

—My good woman, I forgive you, for you are lost in a dream. Your folk has run amok. First genocide, now tyranny at the workplace. Let me reassure you, I am not a Semite. But if I were I would be proud. I would hold my head high and fight you to a man.

—I'm goink to call security.

—It will do you no good, for this is my rightful throne. Alan H. is indisposed and has left me in charge of editorial matters. Needless to say, those matters are not your concern. Ask the editorial assistant, she will know. I believe he left a message on her machine. Now please go tend to your routine duties, and leave me to man the helm of this great ship. You, madame, closely resemble the Lorelei. I am referring to the rock, of course, not the seductive maidens singing to sailors. Away with you, Lohengrin! Take your collective guilt and begone.

—Zat's it. I'm callink.

12:44

While the bathtub was filling she knelt down and examined its clawfeet. The blind dog had followed her into the bathroom and was lying on the mat with its chin on its paws. She compared. The feet of the bathtub were hairless and smooth, an arched exaggeration of feet. Not dog feet but lion feet, the feet of wild predators not domestic pets. Lions without claws: the feet of a declawed lion. There were clawfoot chairs and couches. Bankers, lawyers, doctors sat, bathed and lounged on the disembodied feet of beasts. She stroked a cold foot and then stopped.

Poor beasts.

—Is furniture just furniture? she asked the dog, but his ears did not move.

When the bathtub was full she turned off the water, peeled off Ernie's shirt and stepped in. She had always loved water, contained or boundless as it could seem. She laid her head back carefully, carefully placed her arms beside her, slowly let them sink beneath the surface. Then her head, very slowly, until the water was over her nose, eyebrows, hair.

Lola twirled on a dance floor in her crinoline, kind, kind, faultlessly kind but ignoring the world. Little girl in the morgue. Happy mother. Mummy in a Dumpster.

At Ray's burial there would be fake flowers and her mother standing beside Linda Tulip Johnson, a/k/a LTJ: friend, hairstylist and Seventh Day Adventist. Afterward they would take off their shoes to let their nylon-covered feet breathe for once. They would put their feet up and watch the TV preachers. Around them unnoticed the lakes and the forests were turning into fields and the fields turning to minimalls, parking lots, and highways.

And she had watched the vendor go. Probably all he wanted was what she did, not to be alone. But she had not answered him. No one had helped. All she ever did was dream of the self she could not be, dream she was swimming, dream she was running, dream. She loved the dream. But it was only a lullaby.

When what it should be was the fire of waking life.

She had been wrong in all of it, the rope without anchor. Under the water she felt frozen and held, a warming amber enclosing her. She was malleable.

I should have done it all differently. In apology things melted, merciful. Could you apologize forever? Only by going away.

Her head was hurting, her lungs burned from holding her breath. Is anyone there? Just one! Just one!

Then there was an answer. A touch of her knee. Someone had come! A sand dollar, hundreds of miles from the sea. She burst above the surface, choking, sputtering and coughing, hopeful and grateful.

It was a rubber duckling.

1:03

—You gotta leave now. And the little guy too.

There were two of them, ham-eating layabouts with nothing in their futures but minimum wage and then a gangsta rap album that went platinum in six weeks.

—You do not understand, my musclebound brothers. Alan H. left me in charge.

—Stop with the bullshit, said the jailbait editorial assistant, poking her brunette head around the doorjamb. — Jesus! What happened to you? Get beat up? You look like shit. You know you've got a bald spot on the side of your head. And get those bloody fingers off the desk.

—He left a message on your machine, did he not? queried Decetes staunchly. Out of the corner of his eye he saw Ken deflating the love doll surreptitiously, kneeling on her legs to press out the air.

—Do you think I'm an idiot? That was you.

—Then where is Alan, my likely lass?

—Sick I guess, hung over, whatever, but don't you worry about it because it's none of your goddamn business. Just get out. If he finds you in his office he'll hit the roof.

—Ah but that will not occur, quoth Decetes most sagely, and laid his finger alongside his nose, Santa Claus style. —I tell you what. You have my number in your fine Rolodex. If Alan fails to show, you certainly know who to call. For I will save the day. As indeed I save all days, for I am the redeemer.

—Cut the crap, you loser. Lew, move 'em out.

1:10

In the bathroom, whose floor was wet from water rippling over the rim of the clawfoot basin, Alice sat holding the rubber duck and laughed until she could finally cry.

1:11

After he called Animal Control Phillip sat down on the sofa to await their arrival. He was very late for work: these were indeed the times that tried men's souls. But his moral responsibility was to the welfare of the citizenry first and foremost. Averting the Bubonic Plague surely came under that heading.

It was a welcome delay in any case, for the situation at the office could only be delicate in the extreme. Phillip made himself a cup of organic herbal tea, Peppermint. Would the painted harlot dare to show her face at Statistical Diagnostics? Would she taunt him silently in the knowledge that his kidnapped soon-to-be-former wife was held hostage in her own domicile? He must determine the precise form of all negotiations leading to her surrender. Still, this might be difficult to engineer, beneath the watchful prying eyes of office personnel.

More crucial still, which face would she show him today? It might be the cold and casual aspect with which he was all too familiar. Or it could be—there was only a small probability of this, but significant all the same—it could be the face of the shy virgin, peeking from behind the other mask.

The doorbell. His tea was already cold. He opened it. A short pale man with frizzy hair.

—Animal Control sir. We saw the animal on our way up and we're disposing of it for you.

—It's not mine! My neighbor—

—We don't usually deal with hamsters unless they're rabid, which I don't need to tell you is extremely rare, but we were in the area. Just wanted to let you know it's been taken care of.

The man was already turning away.

—But the bubo. The festering growth on its bottom. Is it contagious? It was just like the rats in medieval Europe.

—Sir that's a male hamster. Are you familiar with hamsters?

—I do not favor rodents, domestic or otherwise.

—It's a normal male hamster. It doesn't have a growth. Probably died of a heart attack.

—But I saw—!

—Sir, those were its testicles.

1:20

He was an Ascetic and a Saint of Self-Denial. She should have known all the time. He was a Holy Man who walked Humbly, not in poverty but in moderation. He had taken vows of Chastity. Not wishing to draw attention to himself, he was quiet in his calling, which was why, until now, she hadn't known. He trusted her implicitly he said. He said he could rely on her Discretion.

Abelard and Heloise lived separately with a Gulf between them, due to the fact that her uncle the Canon emasculated him by cutting off his Parts, but they shared a Great Sacred Tragic Love. They were pure and very very pious and after their secret marriage they lived forever apart only to be reunited in Kingdom Come, plus they were buried together in France. Probably in Kingdom Come he got his Parts back, like for example when she herself was in Kingdom Come she would have flowing shining hair and a flawless complexion, because in Kingdom Come the holy became what they were Inside. For instance she Bucella would be flowing and shining, but Alice, if she even got there in the first place, would be unattractive for Poetic Justice.

So that was the reason. Ernest was a hermit like Abelard. They said Abelard was a Heretic so then he wrote the story of his Misfortunes. True it was in the twelfth century when there were solitary abbeys and horses galloping at night and wild forests and the earth was the center of Everything and the stars were the eyes of God in their millions, and there were Martyrs and Queens and Pageants, undiscovered seas and mountains, but that didn't mean it couldn't happen now.

They tried to make you think it couldn't, by their dirty ugly cars on the freeway, talk shows of ladies with spiky eyelashes and pink boots and puffy hair, by the IRS and social security numbers and dry cleaners and gas stations and I FUCKED YER SISTER and CHILD MOLESTER and Garfield the fat stupid cat and *Sodomania* and prophylactics under the couch and four-eyed Mentals vomiting lasagna on the carpet and garden gnomes and Dean poking his Pecker inside the Lost Souls.

The pamphlet! She opened her desk drawer. The address was a P.O. box in Santa something which was no doubt extremely picturesque. It was in Fields, surrounded by wild-flowers. They made honey there and every year she mail-ordered several containers on her Mastercard. They had many kinds such as clover, strawberry, chive honey and ginger honey, even licorice honey but that was not appealing to her personally. When they were kids Dean once ate nineteen bags of Twizzlers in front of her on a dare from some bully kid and she could never look a Twizzler in the face again.

It was mysterious how they put the flavors in. Once she asked them on the phone how they did it, whether they fed the bees chives or whatever, and the phone woman said, *It's certainly a mystery!*, so it was still a mystery.

She was an excellent customer, which they would certainly appreciate and it would count in her favor. She rummaged until she found it. There! A telephone number for ordering. Poverty, Chastity, Obedience. She once sent away for information on another one in Latrobe Pennsylvania, and also Servants of the Blessed Sacrament in Waterville Maine, before she met Ernest, but this one was more romantic and had a better climate plus Pennsylvania was far away. She and Ernest had an Understanding and the way was clear, it was a shining road strewn with Roses, she didn't even know if it was Benedictine, Dominican, Franciscan or Carmelite and hopefully it wasn't Trappist or Cistercian so she wouldn't have to be a Vegetarian or wear bare feet but if she had to she would, since that was not the Point.

Glory! They could write letters, which might even go down in History because they would bespeak a Great Sacred Tragic Love.

—Here are your nylons Ernie.

—Alice why don't you close my door and help me choose hair accessories.

—Ernest?

Bucella Decetes stood in the doorway, prim and stiff.

—Yes Bucella, may I help you?

—Excuse me, I'm leaving for the day. I sent you the last Iowa PSU age-structure mortality file.

—Go ahead Bucella. Everyone else is doing it.

—Yes. Thank you. Just so you know, Phillip's wife is staying with me temporarily. He may be upset when he comes in.

—So you two hit it off?

—Hardly Alice, said Bucella, pursing her lips. —She is very challenged. I am offering a helping hand.

—Teaching her the scriptures?

—Preventing spousal abuse, said Bucella, and turned on her heel.

—Oh my, said Ernie. —I find that hard to believe.

—Most underreported crime in America, said Alice.

—So what do you think, the barrettes or a hairband?

—Neither Ernie. Keep it simple. I have to go send flowers to my mother.

1:45

He had decided on a stealth approach, both to Statistical Diagnostics and to the harlot herself: the only viable option. To that end he waited in his parking space for her cigarette break. When she came out the front door he followed her on foot for four blocks: then she entered a flower shop, and he waited in the shadow of an awning. After she emerged from the florist's she looked up at the sky and then stooped her shoulders to light her cigarette. Soon, flattened underfoot, that foul cancer stick would become a butt smeared with pink and crawling with miniscule germs: a public nuisance. The mouth was notorious for its virulence. He himself brushed vigorously and gargled antiseptic Listerine six times daily. Caries would find no purchase in his molars. Nor viral agents in his tonsils. Still, her penchant for cigarettes was currently the last of his concerns. The first was to unveil her, before she reached the office. Force the shy brides into the light.

He walked softly behind her. She took a shortcut through a paved alley lined with green garbage cans, around which fruitflies were circling. Passing an old floorlamp put out to pasture for the municipal sanitation workers, shade askew, beside a pile of carpet scraps, she drew to a halt and turned to look at it, touching the edging on the shade. As she turned Phillip concealed himself behind a hanging branch. Then she resumed her walk, throwing her cigarette onto the pavement without stubbing it out. He felt her carelessness like a bee sting.

Clearly the dominant personality had charge of her now: a callous, cold strumpet, a blond she-devil sweeping the terrain with her insidious arms, her caramel-colored slim arms that hung now beside her shapely hips swathed in black cloth ah yes the black of witches and of Beelzebub himself: she wore the black cloth as a flag of her impurity. It cradled her weapon, the mouth of the hot and angry volcano where magma flowed and rushed in the underground caverns of the damned, the salty peach of the virgin self turned to filth and entertainment. It hid the mound of naked heathen Venus who spread her legs for all without discernment, even the ancient Greek Sodomites, those Three Tenors for example, pedophiles to a man, lazy European pedophiles with swarthy skin, masquerading as Catholics while they drooled over the buttocks of innocent choirboys and were sponsored by AT&T in the commercials, filling their pockets at the expense of honest hard-working Americans—Venus yes who offered up her succulence to hedonistic revelers in immoral Bacchanalia, her black hips swinging as she walked, a dance of lust and sultry silent whoring performed for passers-by, the dance that lured stalwart men into the dominion of her appetites and then consigned them to exile. She was laughing all the way to the bank, a vulture and a Medusa. She should be gutted like a fish, slit open, penetrated and dismantled, thrown down, forcibly suppressed and manfully violated, stripped of the tools of her guile, plunged and riveted at the core.

Only that would bring the virgins fluttering to air.

It was hazardous, yes. He would be placing himself in peril. His very life was at stake, his own purity in terrible jeopardy. Yet he was acting in defense of the spiritual domain, of the world of decency and sanctuary. He was sacrificing his honor for the protection of the weak, for the pursuit of virtue. Bring the virgin brides to the surface, force off the mask, expose beneath—the wet ripe fruit. The luscious pit. There was a saying for this occasion. —It is a far, far greater thing I do, than I have ever done; it is a far, far better rest that I go to, than I have ever known, he whispered under his breath.

This was the test. He would conquer the earthly by courage and will, quell matter by dint of his spirit's resolve.

She stopped again and leaned up to pick a blossom from a trailing bougainvillea, precisely as Eve had plucked the apple. He could feel her influence already. She pretended to be unaware of him as he gained on her from behind, but her vice was touching him in tentacles of scent, brushing against him with crass caresses. Blood was rushing to his extremities. He was engorged. *Oh yes.* The python strained against fabric. Still this baseness was necessary if he was to triumph. He was wielding the spear of righteousness. It felt good, oh it was good. It pressed him onward. It steeled him for the surge. Penetration was imminent. He walked faster. It resisted containment. It was a dog of war. It pulsed and pushed, feeling the teeth of the zipper. Rule, extirpate. He was running. The fabric brushed against it, again and again, with his strides. Oh my yes. But wait.

—Phil? What—

She had turned. The pink lips for sucking. The edge of a breast, luscious, with a sharp tip—sharp tips—red tip. Ah no. No! The surge! He stumbled and tripped, covering his groin with his hands. The spasm. Beyond control. Another. Wetness. Sticky on the cotton. He was dizzy. Lights in his eyes. He crashed against a wood fence and fell, uncupping his hands and raising his elbows to shield his face.

—Phil? Are you okay? Do you need help?

—Get away from me! he choked, eyes squeezed shut.

—Are you sick to your stomach?

With the palms of his hands he could feel the fabric. Not wet on the outside. Shame invisible on the surface. At least safe from that. Not visible. The underwear. Thank God.

—Where is my wife? Where is she?

—Phil? I have no idea where your wife is.

—Liar, he said. Oh no. Tears in his eyes, the shame filling them. Stop! Betrayed again by meat. —I found your note. The second note. Don't lie just tell me where she is.

—Phil I didn't write you any note. Take my hand, let me help you up. I think you're confused. It's the nausea, it makes you dizzy. Just let me help you up.

—You liar! Where's my wife?

—No wait. I do know. I remember! She's staying with Bucella. Phil—is there anything I can do?

2:16

The man at the Salvation Army stared at his clipboard, flipped over the top page and shook his head. —Sorry lady but you gotta schedule the pickup aheada time. We can maybe do it the end of the week. All the trucks got routes. They got preassigned routes from the schedule. You see there? We only got two of the big trucks.

She had to do it today, for it was a grand Gesture that would start the ball rolling. It was the Momentum she needed. She was beginning afresh and no Worldly Possessions could deter her purpose. She would throw herself into the arms of the Mother Superior carrying only a suitcase and tell them how she gave it all up, even the spice rack that was carefully organized and her collection of Love Is . . . and Precious Moments plates and figurines, and they would have to let her in because she would be Poor. She would be alone and poor in this world, except for the Sacred Tragic Love with Ernest and her Faith.

—I would like to speak with your supervisor.

—Help yourself lady, she'll tell you what I told you. Back there.

She passed many elderly women picking at bins of used clothing and knocked on the door at the back.

—Yeah it's open.

—Excuse me but are you the supervisor?

It was another old lady, with glasses and dyed magenta hair. The gray was showing at the roots.

—What can I do you for.

—It's very important, I couldn't call ahead for personal reasons to schedule a pickup but I really need one of the big trucks to come to my house today and take all my material possessions. I promise it's worth it. Some of them are quite valuable and the furniture is in excellent condition.

—Sorry but they're already out on their rounds. Maybe nearer the end of the week.

—No please, you have to help me. It has to be today. Tomorrow I am entering the service of the Lord.

The supervisor took off her glasses and rubbed the lenses with a balled-up Kleenex from the pocket of her yellow pants.

—Where do you live?

—Culver City.

—Lemme take a look at the routes. I'll be back in a minute. Have a seat while you wait.

Bucella perched on the edge of a plastic chair, knees together, hands on her purse. On the wall was a calendar with deers on it in the snow. There was a framed service award and the gray metal desk was covered in papers and a white coffee mug that said #1 MOM.

Anyway the children of #1 MOM became graffiti artists and drug dealers and impregnated twelve-year-old girls. They sat and watched television while #1 MOM was at work and their heads were filled with senseless violence and if they didn't deal Drugs, buy Guns and shoot each other Dead in the street in a gang war or spend all their time playing videogames where all they did was blow up things then they were adults and turned into electricians, computer programmers or insurance claims adjusters with no vision of a Great Sacred Tragic Love.

While the #1 MOMs were churning out their bank tellers and software engineers and shoplifters and Drug addicts and serial rapists driven mad by the noise of the city and the litter in the gutters and the spread-legged fallen women in Dean's filthy magazines, she Bucella and her holy sisters would be living chastely in the Field of Flowers, farming their bees and waiting patiently for the day when all the machines were gone, the concrete was gone, the smog was dispersed, the rapists slept in cemeteries nationwide and there was no more I FUCKED or CHILD MOLESTER and no more highways or ITT Tech commercials or music full of *bitch this* and *motherfucking that* and no more pubescent boys in baggy jeans, boys that had just been sweet little babies a short time ago, swearing on the sidewalk and drinking malt liquor from wrinkled paper bags.

And also there would not be fathers leaving little boys in the kitchen in funeral suits who loved their mothers so much that they slept all night in the bed with her crying, when she was already dead.

Bucella would hear the matins bells and cross the cobble-stone courtyard in her serene robes, Meditate in small rooms like Julian of Norwich with the Light streaming in, they would write letters at night with a single candle burning on old wooden desks, they would eat quietly in halls of Arches and sing Hymns. They would wait there until all that was Wrong was washed away in the cool rain of Jesus's tears.

—Good news, looks like we may be able to work you in. One of the trucks rejected a dinette set, he's driving pretty empty and he's right around Centinela now so he should be able to swing by in about an hour.

All would be well, and all manner of things would be well.

3:02

Unworthy. The mistake—but it was honest. He had wanted to see virtue where there was only pitch. Yes, pitch. His first anger had been righteous.

She was nothing to him. Common dirt.

The other woman had Barbara. The busty Catholic. She was to blame for all this: hence her overtures, the dinner and always something at work. Begging and bothering. Clearly she was nurturing an obsession with him, a pitifully inappropriate lust. Understandable but of course completely disgusting. He would set her straight and then reclaim his wife.

He drove quickly, running a stop sign. Possibly Barbara could still be brought into line. He had dismissed her prematurely. She was a work in progress, that was all.

3:33

Unceremoniously expelled from paradise.

Expulsion was becoming predictable, and as such a rhythm as regular as tides. First The Quiet Man, then Bucella, now this. Bucella was chief culprit. She at least should know better.

He sat beside Ken on the parking lot, drinking in the shadow of a chain-link fence. Ken had stuffed the deflated love doll, a pink plastic bundle, into his pants before they left HQ. No small feat of dexterity. Now he was blowing her up again. She took her shape awkwardly, head angled into the sand.

—Ken! The camcorder!

—Sorry I forgot it Decetes.

His kingdom, traded for a horse.

—Damn it Ken! After all we went through to get the damn thing! How will we make the movie of my life?

—So what, you're just a liar Decetes.

Mutiny. Swords and plowshares!

—What are you saying Ken?

—You're just a liar like the public defender.

Ken had stopped blowing. He cradled the love doll against his chest.

—Them's fightin' words Ken. Far be it from me to defend the public. Explain what you mean.

—You said I would meet July: Jezebel. But I never did. You don't even know July: Jezebel I bet. You're a nobody is all.

The worm had turned.

—You don't understand the politics here. You know not, Ken, whereof you speak. July: Jezebel is out of town right now. That's just the way it is. She's on a shoot in Vegas right now. But I tell you what Ken.

—Oh yeah what.

—You like my sister, don't you Ken?

—Yeah I guess. Big bazooms.

—Well Ken, I have a secret to tell you.

—What?

—She likes you too.

—She does?

—She does Ken. She whispered it to me this morning. My sister would like nothing better, Ken, than for you to press your suit upon her.

—Press—?

—She wants you Ken. If you go now, you may find her at home for lunch. Ken, don't take no for an answer. Whatever she says Ken, she wants you.

—Geez!

Two birds with one stone. Bucella would swat away the poor dwarf like a fly, but not without a fit of pique.

3:59

They were fighting and this time it was a big one. They started after breakfast when her mother said couldn't he be late just this once because they needed to have a discussion.

First she tried putting on her Sony Discman and cranking up the volume but she got a headache. Then she phoned Mitch because he was always cutting class, he was never at school so he wouldn't know about the scene with her mother so she could actually face him, but she only got his answering machine. She was sick of her room. She put on her Discman again so they would think she couldn't hear and opened the door.

They were in the bedroom but the door was cracked open. She only saw the chest of drawers with the vase of silver spray-painted pussy willows on it and her dad's suit in slow passes of gray as he paced back and forth behind the door.

—Forget the counselor Riva the guy's a schmuck and it's not doing any fuckin good, he said.

—Well then what are you saying Jerry? asked her mother in a whiny voice.

At breakfast she'd already been wearing normal clothes or at least normal for her, not the gross robe for once, plus she was wearing that wack blue eyeshadow and the disgusting Paloma Picasso perfume. That was a tipoff that something was up.

—I mean Jerry, *you're* the one that can't—

—What I'm saying Riva is once Ginny's gone off to school I think it would be best if we separated and thought about getting a divorce.

3 - 1 = 1. Her mother was left behind like old trash because she was so pathetic.

He was a mean asshole but he always wore a suit and acted normal so he thought he was hot shit. Who kept their trash? No one.

She took the stairs three at a time and then the ones to the basement and ran outside, slamming the sliding door behind her. She crossed the patio and the grass and went to the very back of the yard, where there was the picnic table to sit on beneath the avocado tree. It was the furthest possible away. Now she could play the Discman at regular volume which wouldn't give her that ringing in her ears.

But there was a pang in her like a cramp. Maybe she was also a mean asshole since she thought bad stuff about her mother. Such as secretly wanting the Terminator to blow her head off with a submachine gun. That was not too nice. Even though the bullets turned out to be blanks. If her mother knew that thought, her feelings might be hurt. Luckily she didn't know it and she never would. But also she always made her mother feel bad to her face. It was true she was irritating and stupid but she couldn't help it.

There was a little blue tent in the pervert's backyard between the trees at the back, and a geeky-looking cross-eyed lady was sitting on the ground in a wack bikini in front of it. Reading a magazine. Barely five feet away. Maybe her parents were splitting but at least she wasn't an ugly cross-eyed lady reading a magazine.

She climbed onto the table, crossed her legs, turned on Britney and closed her eyes. To make things even she thought of the Terminator mowing down her dad. With him the bullets were also blanks. But then the Bad Terminator turned and aimed his grenade launcher from the shoulder and blew up her dad's car. That was real. Her dad screamed and ran around squawking and gobbling like a turkey.

Now the geeky lady was gone and there was a little man lying there, naked on his back without moving. How weird was that.

—Ginny? yelled her father from the back door. —I need to talk to you. Ginny honey? Can we have a talk?

Squawk gobble gobble.

4:24

It was a sports bar, but empty save for Decetes. No heavyset warriors beating their shields, no cymbals ringing out as combatants hacked at each other with axes, no flaxen-haired Viking maidens striking their breasts in appreciative blood-lust. Bear-baiting in Valhalla was reserved for weekends. Instead, a dim brown torpor reigned and the TV behind the bar was tuned to local news.

Decetes toasted the whiskey itself. No other toast occurred to him. —Whither thou goest, he told it, —I also go.

But it had a sour taste. Decetes complained to the barkeep and got a second glass free, from a new bottle. It tasted just the same. The stench of rotten lemons, old skin decaying.

The rolling tides cast him again and again on cold shores. California was turning arctic. Even in the hot sun he shivered: walking on the sidewalk after Ken left, he had felt the sun on his shoulders and back but the cold crept over him from his waist, burning like ice. And bright buildings falling into shadow as he walked. Snow-blind in the City of Angels.

Skin decaying. Where had he smelled it? Wide bed, low, soft, sagging in the middle, no spine left. Both of their weights, his slight behind her. She made a bigger dent, he was tipping into it, he was close. Thin orange curtains in the window and the sun going down. *Tell a story okay. Okay a story?* He was the prince in stories, always. No answer. Round slumped shoulder in the dirty flannel: on it a pattern of—what was it? He squinted and almost saw. Ducks? Ducks! Blue ducks. Also ducks! The first ducks. Long ago. Touched the shoulder through flannel. She wasn't warm anymore. — Bucella, he said, —she isn't warm anymore.

—Sir?

—Nothing!

Shut the fuck up. Said the old man.

—Ready for another there?

—There's something wrong with this whiskey. Tastes like something rotten.

—Then why are you drinking it?

Behind the barkeep on the TV they trundled a man quickly by on a stretcher. In the background, an alley and a Dumpster. The headline said *Beverly Hills Murder.*

—Turn it up! said Decetes. —Quick!

A John Doe in Beverly Hills, they said. Wrapped up like a mummy. Strangled.

Suddenly he knew. As if the archangel Gabriel sang.

5:04

She would drop the canned goods at the twenty-four-hour Vons for the food drive. She would work all afternoon and night packing and in the morning the Great Adventure would begin. She could sell the car when she got there. Dean was forty and that was high time to leave home. She would box up his possessions and put them in the front yard.

The front door was unlocked and standing ajar. Dean. She dropped her purse on a chair in the entry hall. Lordy! There was a nude Blowup Doll upside-down on the floor. Terrorism.

She dragged it by the hand onto the front porch and left it there for him, locking the door behind her, and tied on her KISS THE COOK apron. It didn't matter if the neighbors saw the Blowup Doll because she wasn't going to live there anymore anyway.

First she would remove her books from the shelves, the linens from the beds and the files from the cabinets. The Army might arrive at any time.

—But but but, said Barbara, entering the kitchen in a bikini and Dean's wraparound sunglasses that he got free at a downtown street fair from Budweiser.

—Good Lord. Put on your slacks! Right now, Barbara. I am preparing to enter the service of the Lord.

—But but but—

—Please, Barbara. You put your clothes on and then we can have a conversation.

—But, and she turned and shuffled out again.

The last of her Burdens. Barbara, too, would have to fend for herself. Bucella could no longer be a crutch for the Weak. She had a higher calling. Being a Mental Barbara was slow on the uptake, but in due course even the Blind could learn to walk alone.

Bucella lined the spices up in order on the kitchen table. No perishables for the Army. Mrs. Frenter did not deserve them, but Charity was Charity and always commendable no matter how unworthy its Objects.

—You have to come see, said Barbara, reappearing, thank the Lord, fully clothed. —The little guy's down.

—Little guy? I am very busy Barbara, as you may notice.

—He's not moving. At all. Not moving!

—Barbara, I do not understand. Are you referring to your dog again?

—Come on, said Barbara impatiently, and tugged at Bucella's sleeve.

—All right. But quickly. I am busy Barbara.

She followed Barbara out to the backyard. Behind the screen of trees at the back was her Nature Retreat tent. Darn that Dean. She would give that away too. Barbara motioned behind it with her head. Bucella stepped over a pile of clothing and craned her neck. It was the Philistine Midget, nude as a newborn, flat on his back on the ground.

He was unpleasantly hairy.

—Lordy Lord Barbara, what is this?

—Phillip hit him on the head.

—And where is Phillip now?

—Ran away.

—My God!

Barbara took off the sunglasses and bent over.

—Ugly! she exclaimed.

—Hush. God made all creatures great and small. Go get a blanket please Barbara. Run! He could be catching a cold.

When Barbara had turned away Bucella shook the Midget by the shoulders. His mouth fell open. She placed two fingers beneath one of his ears. She felt no beat.

—Lordy Lord God.

Another Tribulation. Who should she call? Phillip had done it. Animal Abuse and Domestic Violence led directly to this. Alice would know what to do. She knew the Lowlifes and the Criminal Element. Bucella ran into the house after Barbara, grabbed the phone and dialed.

—Alice please, I need your help. There is a small dead man in my yard and Phillip is apparently to blame. Please come over.

—Don't play with me Bucella. It's been a long week.

—Alice I am not joking. It is serious. He's an acquaintance of my brother's. I think he is deceased. I cannot detect a pulse.

—Call 911, said Alice. —I'll be there as soon as I can.

Bucella was flustered. Palpitations. It was certainly a Sign. She must remove herself from this world of Turmoil. This Tragedy made it all the more obvious.

In the doorway Barbara was struggling with a flannel sheet, which seemed to be wrapped around her legs.

—I said a blanket Barbara, but that will have to do. Anyway he is dead.

Chapter the Tenth

The Moon rises; an Honest Man takes to the hills; the path to Glory is chosen; and the Salvation Army arrives

Two cop cars were parked out front, lights still flashing, and two vans, Coroner and LAPD Crime Scene Unit. Alice made her way down the drive. Neighbors lined the fences, staring. A teenage girl in earphones blew a green bubble and popped it loudly. The man next to her, in a gray suit, cradled a cell phone between chin and shoulder and gestured as he talked. She caught a glimpse of a bright plastic Santa Claus peeping from beneath a garbage-can lid, and then a crowd scene. In the backyard cops were milling around, stretching yellow tape from tree to tree, a wall of them at the back of the yard beside a small tent. Bucella stood talking to a detective, wearing an apron that proclaimed KISS THE COOK.

—I was not an eyewitness to anything! said Bucella as Alice rounded the corner of the house. —I was in the middle of packing. Tomorrow I am entering the service of the Lord. I am preparing to leave. I am giving away my worldly goods.

—Well you'll have to delay ma'am. This may be the scene of a crime.

—But I had nothing to do with it! He's a friend of my brother's. From AA. His family's in Orange County I think. I only met him yesterday. My brother is an alcoholic and his acquaintances are unreliable. He slept here last night. Only because Dean begged and out of charity I said yes. Then this morning he crept into my room and he, well, *exposed* himself to me. And that's putting it delicately Officer. He was a pervert. I kicked them both out. This has nothing to do with me!

—Where's the lady who found him? asked the detective.

—Right there, said Bucella, and pointed.

Alice followed her index finger. Right there, sitting on a lawn chair, was the woman who had twirled half-naked in the street at the party. She was gazing at the sky.

—But that's Phil's wife? blurted Alice. —She was the one—at the—he said there was a fire?

—Name, ma'am?

—Her name's Barbara Kreuz. Babs for short but I think Barbara is more dignified. She also stayed here last night because her husband was abusing her. She is mentally challenged.

—She claims her husband came running in here and hit the guy?

—She does.

—And is her husband, uh challenged too?.

—In a manner of speaking, put in Alice. —I think he's having a nervous breakdown or something. Seizures, I don't know. He's a little unstable.

—This is my co-worker. We are employed with Mr. Kreuz. At Statistical Diagnostics.

—Okay. That's it for now, said the cop, and walked over to Barbara.

—Alice thank you for coming. Someone crushed my azaleas!

—So what happened?

Bucella led her to the foot of the garden, to the tent. It was blocked off with yellow tape.

—You can see from here, said Bucella.

Alice edged up to the fence and craned her neck. A small pale man lay face up on the ground. The cops were leaning over him. A man in a suit was touching the corpse with latex gloves.

—Myocardial infarction, he said, rising from his squat beside the body. —Heart attack. My best guess for now.

—The Salvation Army! said Bucella. —They could be here any minute!

—Salvation—

—To pick up my belongings. I will send Ernest a letter. I mean just—a resignation letter. I am entering the service of the Lord.

—So you said. You weren't kidding?

—I just have to put things in boxes. They could be here any minute.

—Are you sure—?

—Yes Alice, I am sure. Could you watch Barbara? She is a mental and not very strong. I have to keep packing.

Barbara Kreuz was rocking back and forth on the lawn chair, clutching her knees. The detective flipped over a page on his pad as Alice approached.

—Thanks. That's okay. We'll be in touch.

Alice knelt down beside the chair as he turned away and put a hand on Barbara's arm.

—My name is Alice, she said. —I work with your husband too. Are you doing okay?

—She's mean.

—Who?

—*Her*, and she pointed at Bucella. —She keeps saying I'm mental.

—Well, you don't have to listen to her.

—I'm not mental.

—I can see that.

—*She* might be mental, but I'm not. Sometimes I don't talk right that's all, I just forget the words that go in between, see there's a whole syndrome. I had a speech therapist but he said it cost too much.

—Don't worry. Bucella's just a little preoccupied these days.

—It's not nice to call people mental.

—I agree. So you saw Phillip hit him?

Barbara nodded.

—Did Phillip *know* the guy?

She bit her lip and shook her head.

—Why do you think he hit him?

—Mad.

—But why was Phillip mad?

Barbara cocked her head to one side. Her face twisted: she was about to cry.

—It's okay. You'll be fine. We don't have to talk about it if you don't want to.

—Secret! whimpered Barbara.

—Secret?

—Promise!

—I won't say anything.

—We were doing it.

—You and—?

—Little guy. Because I had sunglasses on so I think he thought it was the other one at first because he called me her name. He came back there and got on top of me!

—Oh.

—But then I—see what happened was . . .

—It's okay. Take your time.

—I kinda got on top.

She paused and looked sidelong at Alice, her shoulders hunched slightly. Alice nodded, neutral.

—See I had my sunglasses on. But then the little guy stopped moving. Then Phillip was there and he yelled the lust and covetous and mind of Christ and pushed me over and he slapped him. But not too hard. And then he felt his neck and looked at me and ran down the driveway and he drove away and left me there.

—I see. Did you tell the police?

—But see the little guy—

—What?

—He was already like that.

—Like—?

—Unconscience.

—You mean he died while—?

—I think he got squished.

—Alice! There's a news van out front! called Bucella from the back door.

—Might wanna tell the CSU to hold up on that for now, yelled a cop across the yard. —Gotta heart attack here. Looks like it's not a homicide.

—Come on, said Alice, and took Barbara's arm. Keep her away from birds of prey. —Let's go inside and give your sister a call.

—Okay.

A fire. She remembered her lit Camel, falling between the wooden slats of the front deck. She had never seen it go out.

—You were in a fire the other night? she asked Babs as they walked up the steps.

—Yep, a fire.

—And was, was anyone hurt?

—Nope, no one.

—Did they tell you how it got started?

—Nope not how, but they said where. Under the porch.

You could torch the world just by looking the other way.

6:18

His vision began to blur due to the perspiration seeping into his eyes. He pulled jerkily to the side of the road and parked the rental, rigid in his seat. Murderer! Perdition, calumny. He removed a tissue from his packet and patted at his brow. He must restore himself. Deep breaths.

There was an insect in the vehicle. A long-legged mosquito. It bounced lightly along the slope of the windshield. He folded his tissue neatly and daubed at it, once, twice along the glass, but it was too quick. They were carriers, hosts. Skittering and bouncing, always twitching at the edge of sight.

The law would hold him and press him into servitude. He had to run. He would go far away. That cottage in Montana, his dead father's old shed. He had not been there since he was ten. And now: sanctuary. The key unlocked the door.

The bells were quieting now, pealing gently. A summer afternoon in the country. Summer country. Mountains and leaves. Only the germs of nature to fear, not the gray city's multitudes. Alone and vigilant, alone and free. The bells were gentler now, yes. They chimed faintly.

Barbara was depraved. She was more than unworthy, she was a blemish. From the first time she had made prurient advances to him, in their nuptial bed at the Ramada Inn, he had suspected her for being what she was, not a child, as first she seemed, but an animal. Many had mistaken animals for innocents, and been slain for their error, a lion's fangs in their throat. Animals bit the hands that fed.

Out of the steadfastness of his constitution he had wished to believe in her virtue. Garbed in a flimsy tight nightdress she had beckoned to him, reclining in a manner she no doubt considered suggestive. It was more than embarrassing: it was an offense against good taste.

He had placed a towel over her midsection and explained the situation. —Think of me as your tutor, he had informed her softly. She had been quite sullen for days. She had refused to accompany him on prescheduled historical sightseeing tours, which were included free of charge in the vacation package. Finally, in due course, the nobility of his bearing and rectitude of his purpose became apparent to her. Needless to say she longed to be given the gift of his carnal attentions; that in itself was not surprising. Patrician, his aunt had remarked, and it was apt. If, one day, he felt called upon to propagate his kind, he would resign himself firmly to the task. He had assured her of that. In the meantime, the body must be effaced so that the spirit of the savior could prevail.

She had accepted it mutely, though he suspected her of covert self-abuse. Direct physical evidence had been lacking however.

To find her in a coworker's backyard, copulating! A pig rutting, a swine. His tutelage gone to waste, lost and forgotten. It had been a terrible shock. No upstanding man would deny that his actions had been understandable. Rotten abomination! *Filth!*

And in the alley the defeat, the shame—. Deflected, brought low. The blond slut was a thorn in the flesh, II Corinthians 12:7. An ignominious fall. Yes, that had been the error of his ways: he gave the scheming harlots more credit than they deserved. No more.

The profane servants of the law. He had already been their faultless victim once.

Montana. The shed would require extensive repairs, a generator, wiring, plumbing. It would have to be sanitized for his protection. But when the work was done, peace. There he could chart his course in safety, away from this, from harlots and abominations. A clean start. Logistics? Work freelance via DSL, running regressions, regressions, more regressions. A steady flow. He had done it before and he could do it again. There in the summer country, to remain vigilant. It was always his duty: he was vigilant. He was society's quiet watchdog. Unsung.

The mosquito, thankfully, had migrated. Order would be restored. Henceforth he and only he would be the keeper of the light. No scarlet women would trespass upon him now. *Get thee behind me.*

He would have to return the rental before he left. The train: the anonymous train. Into the rolling hills it would take him, far away. He rolled up his window and drove.

6:33

Decetes wore a cowboy hat he had found on a bus seat. A little the worse for wear, but it added panache. He was an outlaw now. He had to look the part.

He would hold his press conference in his sister's front yard, just before the onset of dusk. A magic hour for light, known to cinematographers as the golden hour, if he remembered correctly from the pass/fail Filmmaking Techniques class at USC. The public spectacle would be her final humiliation: payback for the insults.

But hark! In front of the house, a frenzy of cars and vans. He quickened his step, knapsack bouncing against his side. He pulled down the brim of the hat: a jaunty angle. Police cars. What could this indicate? Yes: Ken had taken his advice. That was the situation. Little Ken had attempted sexual assault, and Bucella had called in the troops.

And then he saw it. A roving TV news van.

He was still cold under the sun, but providence was with him yet. And now in perpetuity, for he would harness the power of the Fourth Estate. The tabloids and the sound bites were his allies now, his buglers and his flagbearers. His stage was set and victory was nigh. From this day onward he would always be a prince, dark shining moment in collective memory. A fragment of the lives of untold watchers in their homes. He was the massed unacted will of millions, gathered in one point of flame. A testament to the impotence of crude institutions. A monument to the folly of the soul's captivity, the final broken triumph over fear. He was the glorious scapegoat.

6:41

Alice left Barbara on the telephone with her sister and stepped outside for a smoke. The news crew was trouping back up the driveway in an exhausted cluster, dragging their feet, casual but disappointed. Myocardial infarction would not make the headlines.

It was her fault, the fire. The fire had been her fault. But no one hurt, not a single one hurt.

It was the first time she had ever been lucky.

Maybe this was it. The new beginning.

Bucella's drunken brother stepped off the sidewalk onto the lawn. He was wearing a cowboy hat with half the brim missing.

—You! he called in the direction of the news crew, and deposited his dirty knapsack on the porch beside Alice, ignoring her.

A cameraman approached.

—Yeah?

—I have an announcement to make. Assemble the reporters.

—Yeah what's that.

—I am guilty of homicide.

—Yeah right, scoffed a cameraman.

—The John Doe in Beverly Hills, in the Dumpster in the alley. They found him wrapped up like a mummy.

The cameraman hoisted his camera slowly onto his shoulder. Behind him a brunette in pancake makeup and a red suit took a microphone out of her bag. Alice moved back into the shade of the roof's overhang, stubbing out her cigarette against the doorjamb. Carefully this time! Carefully.

—Could you repeat that please?

—His name is Alan H. He was the editor of an erotic magazine. I was his employee. He fired me, so I strangled him and dropped him in a Dumpster.

He spoke in a monotone. Lack of affect, remembered Alice from a textbook, characterized the sociopath. She stared at his profile. Unreadable. He appeared to be sober, for once.

—Hey—! called a cop, walking up swiftly with a radio in hand. —What's this?

—This guy's confessing to a murder. We covered it earlier today, that man in the Dumpster off Beverly Drive?

—I will not speak to the police until this taping is complete, said Bucella's brother stiffly.

—Roll the tape, said the brunette, and stepped up with her microphone.

Alice was trapped in the corner, between door and rail. Something scratched at the side of her face. It was a wreath. Pilgrim dolls and acorns, spray-painted gold.

—My name is Dean Decetes. I killed my employer.

7:06

All the cops and everyone had left the backyard in a rush and her dad already went inside again because her mother came to the back door crying. The little man was covered in a sheet but they just left him lying there.

At the gifted school she would have to share a room with someone else. Had to have something to keep out the geek squad.

She grabbed the end of the yellow tape and pulled it off the tree. This was a real POLICE LINE DO NOT CROSS, not the fake kind she got at the store. Real and a souvenir.

7:09

Bucella was putting pastel-colored ceramic figurines into cartons in her bedroom and humming to herself. Alice cleared her throat. Bucella stopped humming and glanced up, preoccupied.

—Alice! Could you finish packing these Love Is . . . statuettes and Precious Moments for me? I have to do the bed linens.

—I have bad news so you may want to prepare yourself for a shock. Okay? Your brother's in the front yard with the news crew and he just confessed to murder on TV.

—Typical. Dean has always been a liar.

Alice watched her fold pillowcases into a laundry basket.

—But—

—Next to falling down drunk it's the thing he does best.

—Bucella he knows the details of the murder. He described the rope the guy was strangled with. They're going to arrest him as soon as he finishes making his statement. Don't you want to go down there? See for yourself?

—My brother is a drunkard but he couldn't murder a fly. It's bravado. He just wants the attention.

Alice watched her peel sheets off the bed.

—Well he's getting it. He described the murder weapon and the cops are already looking for it where he told them to. Thin white cord. He said he thought it was nylon. He told them it was on the floor beside the victim's bed.

—Believe me Alice, whatever he says he never murdered anyone. He won't even hit people back when they hit him. And they do all the time because he asks for it. He gets beaten up practically every day but he never lifts a finger.

—Really.

—He used to go around saving baby birds when they fell out of nests. He tried to stop me putting mothballs in the closet, that's how weird he is Alice. He's a pervert and a drunkard but he wouldn't hurt a fly. All he does is talk mean, he never hit anyone in his life. Could you unplug that cupid lamp?

—In that case Bucella shouldn't you tell that to the cops? Because if they find that rope where he said it was I think he'll go to jail.

—Dean does what he wants. And jail is where he belongs anyway. He's a thief and a public menace. Plus which maybe it'd sober him up. On top of that he'll be homeless by the end of the month. My rent is only paid till then. He doesn't make any money.

Alice stared at her.

—You're going to just let them take him away? You don't want to, uh, say goodbye?

—I'll be downstairs cleaning out the closet while you finish with the Love Is . . . and the Precious Moments.

—Um . . .

—You don't have to keep them separate. Just bring the boxes down when you're done. And thanks for your help Alice. Thank you so much. It means a great deal to me.

She exited carrying her folded pile of sheets and blankets.

7:18

Ginny sat on the grass a few feet away from the dead little man, listening to Puffy on the Discman. She stared at him, waiting for him to get up and walk away. Or maybe that only worked if you wrapped them like a mummy.

Sometimes she almost forgot it was all a bad trip.

Then two cops came back from the front with a stretcher and lifted him by the feet and head with the black sheet over him and put him on it. She watched them take him away. Smaller and smaller to the end of the drive, through the crowd. He was small to begin with and even smaller at the end.

And no one looked as they carried him past.

7:20

Suitcase in hand, laptop case over his shoulder, wearing two London Fog raincoats and a pair of large mirrored sunglasses purchased at a chain drugstore, Phillip paced back and forth along the Amtrak platform. The weight of the suitcase began to strain his right forearm. He put it down beside him and stood with his arms crossed on his chest, turning to look down the tunnel. He glanced at his watch. Twelve minutes remaining until arrival, eighteen until departure. With a forefinger he stroked the skin above his upper lip.

When he had stopped at the domicile to gather his few necessary appointments he had caught a glimpse of his picture, in the metal frame beside his bed, and hurriedly shaved off his mustache.

For Barbara carried a miniature of the same photographic portrait in her pocketbook. He had presented it to her for her birthday—one of a set of twenty-four in three different sizes, for which he had posed at the Westside Pavilion, seated in front of a sky-blue curtain. The image must, by now, be in the hands of the authorities. His appearance had formerly been quite distinctive; but now, without the mustache, he was almost impossible to recognize. Bare-faced, he was markedly less Prussian in aspect. Less regal. The eagles were mere ghostly, translucent figures. Of course, he would let it grow back when he was home free.

Lord God. There was a uniformed policeman approaching him with a swift gait. Retain control. This was the critical juncture. Deny all charges? Or claim self-defense? No. That could be fatal. Simply deny. Deny. Wife cannot be prevailed upon to testify against husband. No other witnesses. Steadfast denial. He clasped his hands in front of him, palms perspiring, then removed the ticket from his breast pocket and pretended to consult it.

—Sir you want to be careful with your portable computer there. Always keep a grip on it. Those things are snatched all the time.

—Thank you Officer. I always try to be cautious.

—Don't know why they make those laptop carrying bags so obvious. Got the logo right there clear as day. You can spot it a mile away. Worst thing they could do. Just advertisement to thieves.

—I have wondered that myself.

—Worth what, two thousand bucks? And highly portable. What do they weigh, like three pounds?

—It's very lightweight.

—Not as bad here as on commuter trains though. That's where they mostly get grabbed.

—Thank you for your concern, Officer. I will certainly be on the lookout.

The long whine of the train. Thank goodness. They were still running on time.

7:28

—I will grant more interviews, said Decetes into the mic,—at a later date. But as to motive, I can give it to you in one word, and than word is *oppression*. The way I saw it, by killing my unjust employer I was defending the dignity of the exploited everywhere.

Over the heads of his people he caught a glimpse of two sturdy figures walking down the street to a parked car. Their backs were to him and their heads were down; the taller figure had her arm around the shoulders of the shorter. But then they turned and one of them looked back at him as she opened the car door. It was the woman who had worn the skirt patterned with ducks. That same night all had first been revealed to him, a banner in the vast night sky. All that would soothe him, all that he required, was immortality.

Was it so much to ask?

The ducks were a message: I am your mother still, from beyond the grave. I will always be your mother. Her faint and glowing presence was a gentle kiss on the forehead, the ones she used to give when she tucked him in.

And the little prince lived happily ever after.

—Get him outta there, what a fucking pathetic display, said a cop in plainclothes, —you better not run a single fucking frame of this Marty, and the law surged forward in waves, rudely pushing the press corps out of its path.

Decetes leaned forward into the microphone as it wavered and fell away.

—I have never been a violent man.

7:34

Alice came out the door in time to see three cops hustling Bucella's brother into a squad car, hands pushing down on the top of his head to clear the door. He offered no resistance, and a TV cameraman squatted down to film through the back-door window. All along the street, people were staring from their lawns.

A little boy raced his Big Wheel along the sidewalk.

—I told you he was a child molester, said a voice to her right.

She looked over and saw Riva Frenter on the next porch, next to the man with the cellular phone. She had a Kleenex bunched in her hand. Her blue mascara was smeared.

—Bullshit Riva, apples and oranges.

—Riva?

—Alice? Alice!

Awkward pause. The man stared at her. Riva rushed down her steps and across the driveway.

—What are *you* doing here?

—I work with Bucella.

—What a coincidence! Can you believe this? That poor woman. Her brother's a *murderer*? I mean how would you *deal* with that?

—As it turns out she's joining a convent.

—Well! That's a little extreme! Oh. That's Jerry. My husband.

—Pleased to meet you, called Alice.

—Yeah. You too.

—So Alice—he murdered his boss?

—I guess so. Bucella says he wouldn't hurt a fly.

—Well she would, wouldn't she. He's a psycho. Take my word for it. A total Peeping Tom. And he *drinks*.

For a second all Alice could think of was the tone of jubilation. *It's a little black girl!* She'd actually never heard as much joy in a voice. All her life and that was the most joy she ever heard. *It's a little black girl!* Relief should be comprehensible, and it was, but still. If she'd just said *It's not my daughter!* Alice could have kept liking her. And now the little black girl was all she ever remembered: the girl dead and asking for life.

But she saw that Riva's eyes were red. And how the husband stood stiffly away, making sure they were separate.

—Is your daughter okay?

—She's fine. She's going to go to a special school for gifteds.

—Do you want to come over? Pack Bucella's stuff with me? It would be a big help.

—Oh, I—okay but I think she's a little, uh, ticked off at me . . .

—You know what? I bet it'll be fine. She could really use a couple more hands.

The businessman was staring at Alice like he'd never seen a blonde before. She took Riva's arm, turned and led her into the house again, the orange sky behind them. The last police car was pulling away from the curb. And called up the stairs as they went in.

—Bucella? I have another volunteer for you.

—Oh—Riva? Well! That's very nice of you. As you can see we have our work cut out.

Bucella put Riva to work on linens and Alice retreated again to catch her breath, wanting a moment of silence. She sat down on the sofa in Bucella's den, where it was quiet. Open boxes of *Reader's Digest*s. A framed print on the wall. *Triptych of the Annunciation, Robert Campin, Flemish, d.1444.* A tired carpenter, a desperate woman and a smug-looking angel.

What was it she hated about people? What they were, and loved what they could be. Herself included.

Far away in space, where there was no gravity, there was a stubborn outrageous molecule of hope, unseen, untouched, spinning. A long, empty range beyond it, making discovery almost impossible.

Before resistance, sympathy.

Walking slowly around the room she let her fingers drag idly over dusty surfaces until she came to a window. Over the silhouette of a dying palm tree, in a backyard beyond the roofs of other houses, she saw the moon rising, small but almost full, early in dusk. A globe without sharpness, white edges blurred into blue by moisture in the atmosphere. Sphere of resolve. Not full, not sharp and not perfect. But shedding a dim reflected light.

She smiled to herself. That was it; that was all. People were alone, and not only the elegant, the well-balanced, and the lovable. No matter who they were, you had to keep them company.

She would go back to the hill country.

7:44

Bucella wandered down the driveway. It was getting dark and there was no one left on the street but a little kid driving his Big Wheel and making *vroom* noises out of his throat. He almost ran into her as she reached the edge of the lawn. But then. Lo and Behold! She could see it approaching.

A great truck cresting the hill. Glory glory! The Salvation Army.

7:50

The cops in the front seat were silent. Decetes closed his eyes and smiled. Now came the three-night miniseries and the docudramas, the sleazebag Hollywood agents vying for his favors. Now came the crowds gathered outside the courthouse and the jury of his peers. They would be sympathetic, no doubt, for despite his lofty educated language and powerful intellect he was a man of the people. His attorney would select a blue-collar jury, mostly male. The temporary insanity of the eternal underdog, the repressed sad victim of trickle-down economics liberated from conscience for a brief kaleidoscopic moment by rage.

No doubt, with the wealth generated by his notoriety, he would be moved in time to a facility where old robber barons languidly played tennis and shared Stolis with the minions of the SEC. Of course, he would shun them socially: for they were his adversaries, and always would be. Until that time, with the advance on his soon-to-be bestselling true crime auto-biography, he could bribe the guards to bring him in Black Label or Glenlivet on the sly. He could laugh now at the small-time schemes of bygone days, of camcorders and credit cards.

Yes: at long last, after years of slow surrender, he had taken advantage of serendipity. He had met with adversity, and from it, armed only with his native guile, had crafted an empire of redemption.

He lifted his cuffed hands over his head in a clasp of victory and spoke.

—A patriot, sir, and an American.

Lydia Millet is the author of three previous novels, *My Happy Life* (Holt, 2002), which won the 2003 PEN-USA Award for Fiction, the political comedy *George Bush, Dark Prince of Love* (Scribner, 2000) and *Omnivores* (Algonquin, 1996). She wrote *Everyone's Pretty* after a stint as the copy editor of *Hustler* magazine in Beverly Hills, California, in the 1990s. She is an essayist and screenwriter as well as a novelist and lives outside Tucson, Arizona, with her husband, conservationist Kieran Suckling, and their daughter Nola.

Coming July 2005

OH PURE AND
RADIANT HEART

LYDIA MILLET

OH PURE AND RADIANT HEART by Lydia Millet

Oh Pure and Radiant Heart picks up the three scientists who were key to the invention of the atom bomb—Robert Oppenheimer, Leo Szilard and Enrico Fermi—as they watch history's first mushroom cloud rise over the desert on July 16th, 1945, and puts them down in modern-day Santa Fe.

One by one, Oppenheimer, Szilard and Fermi are discovered by a shy librarian who becomes convinced of their authenticity. Overwhelmed and seduced by the scientists, whose historical celebrity and personal eccentricity captivate her, she devotes herself to them—to the growing dismay of her husband.

Soon the scientists acquire a sugar daddy, a young pothead millionaire from Tokyo who bankrolls them. Heroes to some, lunatics or con artists to others, and possibly a serious threat to the military-industrial complex, the scientists finally become messianic religious figureheads to fanatics, who believe Oppenheimer to be the Second Coming.

As the scientists gather a cult following that traverses the country in a fleet of RVs on a pilgrimage to demand global nuclear disarmament, they wrestle with the legacy of their invention and their growing fame while Ann and her husband struggle with the strain on their marriage—a personal journey married to a history of thermonuclear weapons.

1-932360-85-9 | Cloth | 6 x 9 | 448pp | $25.00 | Fiction/Literature